Destiny Dawns

By

Raymond Ross

Destiny Dawns
Published and Printed by
Rayross Print Factory
1st Edition printed 2003
2nd Edition printed 2005

Copyright © Ray Ross 2003

96 Duke Street, Liverpool L1 5AG
Tel: 0151 708 0590 Fax: 0151 709 0759
Email: print.factory@virgin.net
Website: www.printfactory.co.uk

Dedication

To my late mother and father, Kitty and Jack Ross. Mum you were thrilled when you read the first five chapters. I would love for you to have read the complete volume. Dad your memory is engrained in some of the chapters and your experiences recorded therein.

A special message to my wife Rosalinde, daughters Rochelle and Olivia, son Jonathan and daughter-in-law Karen. To my mother and father-in-law Yvonne and Leslie Myers. My sister and brother-in-law Melinda and Brian Davies, and niece and nephew Phillip and Francine. My brother-in-law and sister-in-law David and Carol Myers, and niece and nephews, Danielle, Ben and Sam.

All have had to listen to my constant prattle about writing a book and are no doubt glad that its been completed, sentiments I am sure are shared by all my close friends.

I hope you enjoy the book and look out for the next.

Acknowledgements

I am indebted to:

Gill Cohen, Jeff Shulkind and Stephanie Blumenow who expertly proof read the manuscript.

My late aunt Myra and cousin Yonathan who forwarded detailed information from Israel.

Bill Anderson for his recall of cargo liners.

Mr. Eric Simkin and Mr Cecil Moss for their medical advice.

Malka and Bernie Greenberg for their assistance.

BOOK 1

0
Raymond Ross

Chapter 1

As he rounded the corner the tasty aroma floated against him, almost straining to calm his mighty hunger pains now well into their full, two day cycle. Even the crack of the belt, wielded by his father against his back and the clenched fist bruising his already battered body had made little difference to the rumbling and acidic waves that tortured his contracted stomach. The hunger echoed through his body, bouncing from repetition, as yet again he scoured the local corner shops. The butcher and the baker both turned their heads in reply to his cries for help. Alas, sixteen years old, with a tortured frame, skinny and penniless, he could only experience the sweet smells that drifted his way - but today would be different.

On approaching the display of freshly baked rolls mounted like balls of cotton wool his hand automatically, and with reflex precision, clenched its target. Simultaneously his feet sprang into life sending him and his goods forward like a catapult blasting off.

"Stop, thief, stop!" Sam ran, as he had never before, in terror of the chasing hound. His bony feet bouncing the ground as if peddling a cycle and his bare arms thumping the air for balance. The baker's words rang like church bells, waking everyone from their daily chores and nudging the local 'bobby' to life. His whistle followed as it pierced the day in summoning his colleagues' aid.

Sam sped onwards through the narrow terraced streets, weaving through discarded rubbish, round the many corners and mazes that formed the network of his Liverpool neighbourhood.

The bobbies, now numerous, thundered after him; their whistles harmonized their attack as they closed the gap. He was no match for their strength and number, nor could he think clearly. He was doomed, the prison gates coming to life before him and in readiness to suck down his whole being.

***

The universal purchase was lowered onto the netted bales, each one strapped tightly to compress the cotton and to hold its shape. The hook pierced the sling then, with an almighty heave the winch turned. The ropes strained against the pulley blocks as the derrick, supported by the Samson Post, lifted and swung the goods up to the main deck and down the hatch into the hold. Each net housed at least eighteen bales and weighed over a ton. The dockers, armed with hooks, pulled the loaded bales into their holding area to be stacked like cans of sardines, in neat rows and compacted into every inch of available space. This was only the first hold; hold number two was yet to be tackled.

Captain Harris looked out from the Bridge. His crew had prepared the way and now the dockers were busy operating the derricks and winching the cotton aboard. His eyes scanned the shore in expectation of a signal and in worry that the next few hours could bring him into extreme danger. Yet he was content to be exposed to any hazard that lay in his path. After all he was about to be £20,000 the richer on this, his last voyage before retirement.

***

O'Donnell sank deeply into the rear of the taxi seat. The driver kept his eyes fixed glaringly on the road ahead as he attempted to keep his wheels out of the tramlines and away from the oncoming afternoon traffic. From his brown corduroy jacket, O'Donnell slipped out the two long manila envelopes and looked at the contents of the smaller package. His fingers confidently fanned through the sheets of paperwork, the false passport and birth certificate and all the papers he needed for his new identity. He was now a new person, no longer Brady, the hired sharp shooter who only yesterday had gunned down his victim.

Checking the second envelope, he counted the cash for the second time that day before quietly putting both envelopes back in his jacket. 'O'Donnell' he whispered to himself in an effort to remember the name and engrave it into his mind as yet again he was facing the danger he was so accustomed to, the danger that was part of his everyday existence.

"Cold weather again, can't remember the last time the sun shone," announced the taxi driver in some vain attempt to make conversation. "Going far?"

O'Donnell was too deeply focused on his next task to take any notice of the light chatter. He was busy zoning his thoughts into a singular column like the nib of a fountain pen injecting its ink in straight lines. He never wavered and was always exact, just as he would be when deciding which chess piece should be moved and into which square. White Bishop's Pawn to D4, Black King's Pawn to E5. White brings the Queen into an immediate attack. O'Donnell was now ready.

***

Sam ran on; he just had to get away. The police would not look as kindly on him this time as they did on his previous conviction. He had been warned. "Do that again and you'll be put behind bars."

He headed for the only place he could think of as offering some safety, down to the docks. An area he knew well and a place where, with his friends, he had spent many a mischievous time. Down the hill he raced, the docks coming to view and growing with every pace he strode. At the bottom he swerved left into the loading areas where to the right, against the quays, stood the mighty ships. Sam bounced against one package, and then another and another as he tumbled into the harbour's loading bay.

Men were busy loading goods onto the moored shipping giants, waiting to sail against the horizon. His eyes spied large bails of cotton, mounted in netting and certainly large enough to offer some refuge, even if only long enough to recover his breath. The police were moving in as dogs might for the kill. He was trapped, about to surrender and be thrown into prison for the want of food.

The creaking derrick tugged with a great force as it stretched the netting and began to lift the load of cotton bales. Sam held tightly to the strapping when in a sudden motion the goods flew upwards and away leaving the bobbies in wonder as to where he had disappeared. A narrow escape perhaps but most certainly the fire after the frying pan as the derrick lowered him into the hatch.

Suddenly the netting split apart sending its cargo flying down and crashing against the depth of the ship. Sam was thrown to the side as bale upon bale tumbled against the lower deck, the cotton splitting from the strapping and expanding like sponges breathing in air. The fibrous dust immediately swept itself throughout the hold sending the loading dockers up the side ladders for fresh air.

Sam's vision dimmed as fibrous dust spread over him like an angry cloud. The fibre soaked up what little air remained in the hold and, as Sam struggled for his breath, his lungs panicked and his throat reddened into a coughing spasm. Eyes tightly closed, he crawled around, his hands like tentacles guiding his way towards any small mercy. The dust thickened, time was running out. His heart was about to explode.

***

Captain Harris continued his eager lookout, waiting impatiently for the arrival of his passenger, the man he was to escort across the ocean and the man who was to bring him his reward. Harris persistently tapped his wristwatch in chase of its second hand and to urge the minutes to move faster. He just could not bear the long wait. He was in no mood to neither relax due to the tension of his whole being nor calm the pressure that embroiled the circulation of his blood system. The cool air forced itself between the cracks of his buttoned white shirt and against his weighty stomach whose contents leaned over his belted trouser top. Even after 40 years of service to his country and ready to knock on the doorway of retirement, he had not been honoured; no merit given and no golden handshake in sight. He had given up waiting and had chosen to side with the devil in reaching his goal.

The taxi drew close to the quay. The driver sprang out to open the rear door and to offload the luggage. O'Donnell exited the taxi and from his pocket drew out his loose change as payment and reward.

"Thank you sir," the driver muttered with hand stretched out to secure the payment. "Have a pleasant trip." How little did his words mean to O'Donel. This was no pleasure trip; this was the Queen aiming for checkmate.

"Welcome aboard," they shook hands. "Everything is prepared." Harris spoke in a quiet tone so as not to be overheard. "I've processed the paperwork. All we need now is to load the cargo into the second hold and we'll be under way in no time."

"What seems to be the commotion?" enquired O'Donnell. "Oh, just a slight spillage of cotton bales into the first hold. The net must have split apart, probably over weighted by the load. The dockers will soon have it cleared," Harris assured O'Donnell.

The two men proceeded along the main deck towards the bow.

"The cargo is at the far end of the quay. If you look in that direction you'll see the cart being pulled along." The captain pointed towards some old sheds from where the crates of goods were being taken along the berth and to the side of the ship.

"Take care of that load," Harris called as the dockers handled the new cargo. "There are fragile items in those crates. I don't want them falling apart," he continued.

The bow derrick was lowered; the cargo was pulleyed up and swung into the hold for safe carriage. O'Donnell removed the larger of the two envelopes in his pocket and placed it on Harris's hand. "Half now and the balance on completion, as agreed." They both turned and walked towards the passengers' quarters.

"Your cabin is at the far end of the centre section," Harris informed O'Donnell. "Away from the crew. You shouldn't be disturbed."

***

Groping his way along the side of the hold, Sam continued to suffer from the blinding dust and lack of air. Death drew him closer, tantalised with his hopes and toying with his mind whilst all the time encouraging him to succumb to its power. He simply hung on for the very last moment before conceding to the inevitable end. Just as life was closing on him, he stumbled against a number of boxes badly stacked and offering him some refuge. He crawled through the gaps and into a safe area where the dust had failed to penetrate and where the air was still fresh. Some minutes later the dockers returned with their hooks, cleared the spilt mess and continued to load the cargo. Row by row the bales were stacked as before, from wall to wall and floor to ceiling. As the last of the bales were placed into position the men climbed the side ladder, closing the hatch on their exit.

All was quiet. All was dark, not a single flicker of light and in the midst was Sam, barely alive and hanging on to the very edge of life. Exhausted, he lay with not an ounce of strength left in his body and with a deadening pain numbing his bones. Was this the same as being buried alive, six feet under and in a box or was this just another nightmare, similar to the many he had at home?

After all, his father made sure the nightmares continued as he regularly put the belt to him, caned his arms and legs but never once beat him across the head so as to avoid discovery. Then to create more distress, he would attack his mother. She got the worst of his beating and had become bedridden for a good few days.

Friends envied the close relationship Sam and his family had, but they were the only ones being fooled. Little did they know of a bullying father, who spent more time away from home and often in company of other women. Then he would suddenly appear, drunk, swearing and spewing his vulgar ways and that was when Sam's mother suffered the worst of his attacks. She was fragile against his advances and, as much as she loved Sam, she could not protect him from his father.

Sam's mind wandered in circles as he continued to live his nightmare and as he lay in the depths of the ship's deck. He knew that the horrors he was experiencing at that moment did not come with sleep. This one was very real and one that would not end with him waking up.

The last of the bales were placed in the second hold and the hatch battened down. The dockers had now completed their work and had disembarked, allowing the pilot on board to steer the ship through the next difficult procedure, along the harbour. The captain passed instructions to the crew to prepare to sail.

"Let go of the Bow Rope."

The pilot ticked off the first of the list of ropes to be released before the ship could move ahead. The Chief Officer was stationed forehand and the 2nd Officer aft, both supervising and ensuring that all ropes were clear. The pilot was ready and signalled the tugs to come in line and take the slack.

"Half ahead," the Captain ordered the Officer of the Watch who immediately turned the telegraph to half ahead. The Chief Engineer acknowledged, ordering his crew to proceed the steam turbines to power half ahead. As the tugs pulled, the ship moved slowly away from the quayside and the harbour wall. With precise accuracy and good communication between the Pilot and the tugs, the ship was safely steered through the intricate lock systems and into the River Mersey's main flow. In mid- river the tugs released their hold, the Telegraph was turned to full speed and the vessel proceeded to the Bar Light Ship where the Pilot was able to transfer onto the Pilot Cutter and hand the ship back to the Captain.

A south course would take the ship at 12 knots round Anglesey, eventually heading for the Mediterranean.

***

In his quarters, O'Donnell opened his leather case fully to reveal his sparse clothing, folded neatly and located in its individual areas: two shirts, trousers, one jacket, a pair of shoes and a number of smalls. Just what he needed for the short trip to the appointed rendezvous. Carefully he removed the clothes and placed them into the only piece of furniture his tiny cabin contained. His fingers pressed at what seemed to be the base of the case to release the secret lid to the hidden compartment. With the lid open, O'Donnell's eyes lit up at the sight of the automatic laying snugly and peacefully in its nest. The threat that it held was certainly not obvious nor did there seem any danger in its present state of rest. Lovingly, O'Donnell lifted the automatic from its cushioned place and began to caress its long shaft like a child with a favourite toy. He held it to the mirror, pointing at himself and imagining the powerful effect its presence harboured.

His finger fondled the trigger, rubbing at the curved surface and rolling sideways at its rounded edges, the feeling of which he was only too aware, and the scratches of which were well ingrained in his memory. His muscles tightened as they gently awakened the hammer from its resting-place as millimetre by millimetre it rose to its firing position, kicked backwards and then fiercely shot forward at the firing head. The loud click, which would normally have been the explosion of a lethal bullet, was the effect of an empty barrel, one waiting to be loaded for its ultimate target.

The rapping at the door pulled O'Donnell from the trance he was experiencing, a sudden awakening from deep within his floating and oblivious head. Bitterly he looked at the door from behind his wild eyes, angry at being disturbed as a couple would be in the middle of their sexual arousement.

"Who's there"? His voice boomed from between his vocal cords and bounced out like an ace served tennis ball.

"It's the Captain, Mr. O'Donnell. Thought you might like to know our progress." O'Donnell expertly and with a lightning move replaced the gun in the case and removed all evidence of threat and excitement the cabin had previously held.

"Ha, Captain." O'Donnell's teeth beamed as he threw back the cabin door and gaped a welcome. "Come in, Captain. So how are we progressing?"

"The going's fine, full ahead and we should make good time to deliver your goods to Crete and see you safely onto Greek soil. Should be no more than eight days sailing." the Captain was pleased to report.

"Are you happy with your accommodation?" he continued nervously. O'Donnell ticked the days through his head, knowing that he only needed three for his mission.

"Thank you captain, the quarters here are just fine," he replied in a brief and matter-of-fact way not wanting to continue any idle chat. "Now if you don't mind," he continued as he gestured with his hand towards the open door.

The captain parted his lips with some words he was about to dispense when he thought better and decided to back off. After all, he was not about to upset his passenger nor his ultimate reward.

"Well, if there's anything you need, don't hesitate to call for me if you...." His words tapered as he manoeuvred backwards through the exit.

O'Donnell's eyes again focused on the case, his instincts warning him not to overreact. The time had to be right and the moment carefully calculated. The captain had made his move and now O'Donnell's Queen was closing in.

***

Sam's body ached from being folded over and over again, like a piece of paper slotted into a tight crack. He longed to extend his feet, stretch his bones and muscles, and yet he first had to fight the blackness that surrounded him. His pupils were now well dilated, their lenses expanded to capture any image, which might shadow itself before him. Alas, there was no light, not even the slightest glimmer. For all he knew, in front was a black hole waiting to suck him into an eternal dive.

He could, however, feel the sway of the ship and the vibration of the steam motors as they relentlessly rotated the propellers through the flow of the sea. He had no idea how long the ship had been sailing or the time of day. He was not even sure where he was, where he was going and how he would be rescued. However, through all the uncertainty he was aware that, for the moment anyway, he had escaped from the police, from his father's beating and from the life he had come to hate. Even a black hole seemed better than anything he had experienced in his short life. Slowly he unfolded the creases of his body, allowing the blood to flow back into his capillaries, with painful effect of pins and needles stabbing messages through his nerve endings. The numbness that had taken over his entire body awakened its senses and allowed him to once again feel comfort. Using his fingers, he carefully groped along the floor and vainly brought images of the cargo he had seen when he first fell into the hold. His memory pointed to the bales upon bales stacked like huge cylinders, upwards and sideways. No matter which way he turned he bumped into some item of cargo, there seemed no escape from possibly the only area of haven he had tumbled into when he first landed. Considering his situation and resting for a moment, he decided to climb his way to the top of the pile before attempting a sideways move. Fortunately, the straps binding the cargo gave him all the footholds he needed.

The gap between the cylindrical bales was just the right size for a skinny 16 year-old, who for the first time was grateful for his lean body and the lack of food he had learnt to recognize ever since the first day he had held a spoon. Scaling upwards he finally reached the top of the pile and stood to feel for the roof, a gap of some four feet and one that he could use as support for stepping from cargo to cargo. The going was painfully slow and he was not sure the direction he chose was the right one. At the end of the row, he came up against the side and with some relief stopped to recharge his energy. The coldness of the wall suggested to him that he was against the side of the ship, the barrier that held back the force of the ocean from entering. He followed the side of the wall, leaning against it as he moved from cargo top to cargo top, until he reached another wall going at right angles to the first. He reckoned that this was either the front or back of the ship. Suddenly his hands came across a set of pipes, lined up like the steps of a ladder and arranged up the wall as well as down. He believed this to be the ladder the crew used when climbing in and out of the hold. The ceiling was higher at this point and he impatiently climbed up in hope of reaching a doorway to the deck of the ship and to refuge. He

19

was right. The ladder did reach an exit, a closed cover, but one which was locked from the outside.

Like a rampant bull he banged at the cover, pushing and shoving in a wild rage, oblivious to the pain and harm he was causing himself. He slumped down, totally fatigued from his futile attempts to budge the cover. It stood firm, tantalizing and toying with his shameful efforts. There was just no way he was ever going to be able to open the doorway to heaven. He was cooped and trapped in a hole, as if buried alive and waiting to die. In and out of sleep his mind wandered, as he lay exhausted and beaten. Without food or water he was doomed to end his 16 years in a matter of hours. This was the end; there was no hope of survival.

***

The sun dipped into the horizon, letting the night have its way. The sea lapped quietly and calmly against the ship as it speared its way from wave to wave. The night's coolness offered a happy feeling of freshness to the crew members who settled down in their restful mode. They had worked hard the last two sailing days and were entitled to ease down a gear and discharge any tension from within. Except for the few who stood at lookout, the men gathered in the mess to enjoy their moment of rest over food, ale and cards.

Billy had joined the ship's crew some six months before and, at the age of 16 was still very much a novice in the eyes of his workmates. He was the Deck Box, the lowest position any crewmember could achieve and yet he did not mind the constant bullying that came with the work. His eyes were set on a much higher position on the ladder of seniority. He promised himself that one day he would be an officer with a whole string of medals at his side. He loved the sea and always longed to be aboard the great vessels that sailed to far places. But right now, his duty was to run errands for everyone. At the merest wave of a hand, a nod and a wink he had to move double time to the piper's tune. If they said jump, he would jump and if they said run he would run. There was no such avenue as peace. He knew his place and knew that to get to the top he had to start at the bottom.

He sat around the table watching with admiration the Able Bodied Seamen playing poker: drawing, checking, raising, calling and seeing. Words so meaningless on their own, but in poker, he had learnt they were not used lightly but with much thought and deliberation. The use of the wrong word easily threatened the balance of the game and the comfort of the individual.

"I'm going for some fresh air." Billy announced, as if anyone was interested. They were too embroiled in their game to even notice he was in the room let alone hear what he had to say. The door from the mess room led out to a small corridor from which other doors stood guarding the Captain's quarters and other seamen's quarters. He made straight for the deck and as he opened the door, the night hit him full in the face.

Stepping onto the deck the cool air refreshed his senses and temporarily spread a rash of goose pimples throughout his entire body. He walked to his favourite spot, at the far railings where he could eye the glimmer of the curved moon as it shimmered across the calm ocean, which was bouncing lightly at the tiny ripples. The distant, cloudy shadows played on his mind as they endlessly formed new patterns and familiar objects. One minute they looked like coaches being pulled by horses across the sky and the next like crowds of people floating. Tonight's cinema sky screen was showing a new epic, a picture, which with Billy's imagination was as good as any showing in Hollywood.

***

Sam's dehydrated body, whose sand of time had reached the last few grains, lay in a heap, balled up and motionless. Images of his world were spooling through his mind when suddenly a spark of life injected his soul, as if his reflex action was taking control in seeking that last effort of recovery. There just had to be a way out. He gathered his muscles together and with one mighty effort was back on his feet and reaching for the hatch cover. Again, he pressed hard but it would not budge. To get a firmer push he switched his balance to the left side and as he moved, his foot kicked against a metal object. Feverishly he groped through the darkness, with his hands around the area of his feet. He felt a sudden stab of pain as his sore hands pressed against the sharp end of a hook, his mind flashing back to the images of the dockers as they pulled the loads into place. One kind docker had left his hook behind. A crumb of mercy for Sam.

Excitedly he grabbed the handle of the hook and crashed it against the hatch. He hit it repeatedly with all the venom force he could muster.

***

Billy walked back across the deck and decided to use the hatch cover as a temporary seat from where he could continue to gaze at the night. On sitting he instantly felt a throbbing from below, as if something was banging against its structure. He shot upright and looked down.

"Strange," he whispered to himself, "could that be the vibration of the ship's engines?" His thoughts continued. Again he sat down and this time was sure that something was banging from below. His curiosity was so intense that he had to know what was going on. He quickly unfastened the hooks holding the hatch in place and lifted the lid.

Chapter 2

"Assir," I need more steam. We're already half a day late." Hammed
called out to his colleague as he once again looked down at his watch. He
tapped it gently, on the chance that it might be slowing down, but no, the
second hand was skipping along on its never ending journey just as it did
every day.

The fishing boat they had stolen from under the noses of the southern
Spanish authorities, proved to be a little sluggish and probably well past
its sell by date. The wooden hull was well beaten by the relentless
pounding of the waves through its many fishing trips, certainly the glued
smell more than hinted at the presence of fishing holds. Nevertheless the
old boat gave Hammed and his men the sort of camouflage they sought in
accomplishing their task. This was a task which was to reward them for
the rest of their lives, both financially and with the satisfaction of helping
their fellow countrymen in the annihilation of their enemies.

***

O'Donnell sat on the floor, crossing his legs with his feet firmly embedded into the folds of his thighs. He took up the basic Yoga position to close his mind to the world, concentrating on a single item in his meditation and control of respiration. This practice of self-control and complete withdrawal afforded him the best way of mastering his stressful world. He would always assume the Yoga position before entering any episode of danger or closing into a pre-determined target. Five hours to go for the culmination of a plan formulated for many months, developed, nurtured and fostered to a finite degree in its final manipulation.

***

Sam lay lifeless on the Poop Deck. It had taken all of Billy's swift and cool reaction when he lifted the lid and found himself staring at the point of a docker's hook swinging at him. His head dodged the hook, just in time to see it crash against the wooden lid and embed itself. Billy was stunned at the sight of the youngster, with a face crumpled in pain and a body tortured throughout. Billy used all his energy to hoist the young lad out of the hatch and onto the deck. His first reaction was to call the Captain for help, but his instinct made him pause. He had heard the crew talk of stowaways on many occasions with terrible stories of tragedies. If found they would be bound over to face disastrous consequences for their actions. Yet there in front of him, lay this feeble teenager, barely alive and with eyes pleading for mercy.

Billy held back reporting his find and for the moment decided to seek a sheltered area of safety where he could help the boy and clear his own head as to what action he should pursue. He dragged Sam across the deck to the stern of the ship and into the Lazerith area where the steering gears were housed and from where the rudder was operated. This was a small area and one he knew would offer reasonable safety and an undetected resting-place. From the condition and state of Sam, Billy was well aware that he urgently needed him to drink some water. He hurried to his cabin, grabbed a few rations he had tucked away and within minutes was back with the stowaway, holding his head and letting him gently sip liquid.

Billy knew that he had five hours leeway before he was back on duty and this afforded him security from detection. He had plenty of time to decide exactly what direction to take in resolving this situation. At the moment the young boy needed his help and he would stay with him to see the night turn to dawn.

***

The ship made good headway across the gentle expanse of ocean, helped by a clear sky whose stars seem to form a column to guide the vessel. The men on duty went about their work in a very relaxed and casual manner as if in step with the mood of the night, a reflection of a calm and safe atmosphere. Those off duty had reported to their bunks long ago and were well into their dreams of the night, wrestling with thoughts of home and loved ones. Their journey often took them away for many months and to places far away.

No one could forecast or suspect that the ship sailed towards Hammed's boat, like a sleeping volcano whose lava was gently heated for explosion. Even the few instigators could not determine the speed the flow of the molten rock would take nor the heat it would create. The crew did know that the time for action was approaching.

Slowly night turned to day and from the lookout a speck of dust appeared on the horizon. The First Officer was on duty. "Captain," he called down the air-tubes. "Captain," he called again somewhat louder.

Captain Harris noticed 0500 on his watch. He had already been well awake and busy recording the previous day's incidents.

On hearing his title on the air-tube he put down the pen and lifted the mouthpiece. "Yes, First Officer," he said. "What have you to report?"

"There seems to be a fishing boat sailing towards our position," he announced.

"Can you identify the boat?" the Captain enquired.

"No, Captain, she's too far for proper identification, but it's certainly heading in our direction" was the reply.

"Keep watching, I'm on the way." The Captain responded as he hurried from his quarters.

The First Officer eyed the boat down his sights and still could not find any flags or signs of its identity as it continued in their direction.

"Have you tried signalling to the boat?" the Captain enquired as he stepped on to the bridge. "Press the trigger and let's see if we can get some answers," he continued.

The long and short tapping of the trigger head could be heard bouncing along the airways with its Morse letters again and again, repeating the message asking for identification. They stood looking flustered, aware that action might be needed to force the boat to identify itself and satisfy them that they were in no danger. The danger of high sea's piracy, theft and murderous acts were well known in these areas and a constant feature in the world's press.

"Captain, this doesn't look right," observed the First Officer.

"Hold your station. Pass me the sight," ordered the Captain. He snatched the sight to his eyes and looking down the lens was able to view the boat. It was a small fishing boat with no crew in sight, drifting towards them and out of control. And yet it did not seem right to him. Something was missing. He looked for signs of movement on the deck area, a sail flapping or a net being dragged. There was nothing, like a skeleton ship drifting aimlessly. He concentrated on the front where the deck side climbed to the highest point. There seemed to be some rods standing upwards and leaning against the side, like fishing rods but these had no line at the ends and were very short, almost like thin metal tubes. Then it struck him. He lost his balance when he realized they were not fishing rods but rifle shafts being held in place, probably by men hidden behind the side.

***

O'Donnell left his cabin, feeling the power he always sensed before an important meeting of roads. As if at a roundabout, where he controlled the movement and speed of the traffic and where cars could neither enter nor leave without his permission. He wielded his mighty power and on most occasions, those entering the roundabout did so at their peril, circling uncontrollably without ever finding an exit.

The sight of the approaching fishing boat raised his calm temperature a few degrees. His body was well accustomed to sudden changes, always in a mode of expectation and anticipating the slightest threat of danger. Even though boiling point would soon be reached, he would maintain his calmness whilst those around him would easily steam away.

Removing the handgun from its holstered sling he rotated the barrel a couple of times to hear the beauty of the spin and feel the softness of its mechanism. Like holding a woman, he caressed the metal handle and shaft and could feel his sexual desires climaxing. He stood there for a good few minutes to savour his moment and hold on to the adoration and excitement it encompassed. He was ready.

O'Donnell stepped forward, his eyes fixed at the doorway to the bridge, his mind totally focused on the task ahead and his weapon held in readiness at his side. He was the White Queen making the diagonal approach, across the board and onto the bridge. There was no stopping him now, time had run out and destiny had arrived. The Black King was exposed and unprotected, like an animal out of its lair.

***

Captain Harris shot backwards from his sight, his face reddened, his hair standing on end from the shock of what was heading their way. With bellowed lungs he forced air through his windpipe, into the trachea and vocal chords to create a crescendo of sound. Alas before he could be heard, O'Donnell raised his gun, fired one blast and embedded a bullet into the middle of the captain's forehead.

"Checkmate," O'Donnell whispered as the captain exploded backwards onto the deck.

"Perfectly still everyone" commanded O'Donnell as he eyed the First Officer and the three crewmembers on the bridge, his gun pointing menacingly and waving them to a corner where they could be watched. "Your name?"

"Do you mean me?" stuttered the First Officer. O'Donnell nodded.

"Sobers," the officer replied

"OK Sobers, let's move the body out of the way. Come on you two, you can help, or do you want to join him?"

The three crewmen pulled the captain's body to the side and quickly returned to the corner not wanting to chance the end of O'Donnell's barrel.

"Now you," O'Donnell's concentration was directed at Sobers, "you've been promoted to the new captain and I want the engines stopped."

The First Officer sprang to the wheel, gripped the controls tightly and piped down instructions to the engine room. Moments later the ship came to a stop allowing the approaching fishing boat to come alongside.

Ropes thrown across the bow of the ships were hurriedly tied to keep them from drifting. Assir and Hamed followed by the rest of their conspirators, boarded the ship and immediately summoned the crew on deck and forced them to parade in a line alongside the edge of the ship.

"Assir you keep them there, I'm going to see O'Donnell," bellowed Hammed.

O'Donnell held his gun firmly waving at the First Officer to step aside where there would be little chance of retaliation. However, what O'Donnell did not realize was that the warning pistol was clipped to the wall at the corner and within a couple of feet from the officer. On seeing Hammed, O'Donnell turned his gaze for a momentary glance.

"Hammed," O'Donnell announced, "welcome."

Hammed eyed his aide, winked once and tapped his head as if saluting the good work he had done.

"I want everyone out on deck."

O'Donnell waved the pistol at Sobers. "Everyone on deck, and be quick," he commanded. Sobers, with one eye still focused on the warning pistol in the corner took hold of the pipe and echoed instructions for all crew members to go on deck immediately.

"Good, now let's lighten the ship's load," Hammed instructed as he turned to go down to the deck. At the same instant Sobers dived for the wall gun, both hands grabbing at the head, two fingers cocking the firing pin to life and arms swinging the barrel at O'Donnell. In a lightning strike, O'Donnell raised his gun, pulled the trigger and embedded his bullet into the centre of Sobers' brains. Sobers collapsed to the floor in a heap.

The crewmen gathered onto the deck, not realizing the dramatic change in circumstances.

"I am Hammed. The Captain is dead and you will do as I say or be shot. Is that clear?" The men very quickly nodded their agreement whilst stepping a little backwards in a frightened and cowardly way.

"Now lets open the hatch and get rid of the load."

One by one the cotton bales were dropped overboard, they stood out like stepping stones stretched across the sea making a bobbing path over the waves.

"Now the men." Assir pointed his weapon at the crew, and plunged them to the power of the sea and to a certain death. Those who managed to cling onto cotton bales won a moment of reprieve before the waters engulfed their last breaths.

From his hiding place Billy could only watch in terror as the crewmembers were pushed overboard into the perilous waters below, their screams following their fall of death. Billy edged himself into a corner, his eyes transfixed on the ghastly vision and his body motionless in a bid not to be detected. Never had he witnessed such murderous action and seen such terror. Sam was feverishly going in and out of consciousness, not aware of the dangers that loomed, but somehow he had sensed a helping hand slowly guiding him to safety.

The last of the cotton bales were now out of sight and in their shadows remained fragments of strands floating as match sticks on the surface. The crewmen's bodies, some sunken into the ocean's grasp whilst others drifted into darkness, and showing little trace of the murderous horror. The waves looked clean and calm as if satisfied from their feast.

The ship turned east. Billy settled down with Sam's head resting on his lap. The air began to warm from the ovens of the nearing deserts.

Chapter 3

"Sheba, will you hurry up. You're late." Shoshana announced yet again to her daughter. "The bus will be here any minute," she continued.

Sheba hurried through her cupboard, tossing everything to the side in her great effort to find the missing homework. Should she fail to find it, it would be the third time this month and would definitely mean a detention. She searched under the bedclothes, her favourite chair, under the mat and inside the washing basket.

"Oh where can it be?" she muttered to herself, her dress ruffled and every strand of her hair out of place as she raced around her little bedroom. Exhausted, she gave up the search and resigned herself to the mercy of her teacher.

Through the door and down the hall she ran, her mother standing faithfully at the front with her snack bag held high.

"See you later," she managed to announce as she leapt out of the apartment and down the concrete staircase clutching her snack bag.

The sun was only just beginning to peek out from the horizon. Soon the temperature would soar to the 100's and bake everything in its sight. The ground, already cracked from the thirst for water would split further along its seams and shrivel like the peeling of sunburnt skin.

Shoshana rested on the open veranda. She always shed a tear thinking of her 15-year-old daughter going away. She sadly looked at the disappearing bus as it negotiated the long sandy road up the hill and out of sight. Then thoughts of Yehooda replaced the emptiness. Theirs was a teenage romance, taking them through college and sealed by the arrival of their darling baby daughter, Sheba. Yehooda's 6 feet tall, bronzed and masculine body would come to her mind, his face highlighted with bright, ocean blue eyes, guarded by two bushy eyebrows and topped by a smooth and flat forehead. Then she would feel his powerful arms holding her as she snuggled under his chiselled chin. His huge hands would gently caress her breasts, rubbing against her and arousing her inner feelings. She would squeeze him tightly, her hands wrapped round his back, fingers lightly scratching along his backbone, always stopping to tickle his birth mark, a black mole with a distinctive white circular ring towards the centre. The constant border fighting had kept them apart. With busy days and lonely nights her thoughts of their love gave her the strength to continue.

Dr. Shoshana Goodman prepared herself for the hospital.

***

Captain Yehooda Goodman and his elite men, all members of the Israel Defence Force were on special mission. Hidden behind the rocky terrain of the Negev Desert they were at the front line to seek and establish the size and position of terrorist activity. This was as a result of continual terrorist attacks along the road to Eilat.

"Stand your ground," he ordered. He was always the first to take a risk, forever putting his life before those of his men and showing the courage required of a leader. Today was no different, the danger as strong as ever and confrontation imminent. Yehooda left his rock of safety to climb the sand dune ahead and spy on the enemy. Reaching the top he burrowed himself into the soft sand, held his binoculars and blinked at the sight of several tents littered on a small plain. Men were sat around a fire, no doubt preparing food and discussing their plans. In another area one man busied himself cleaning his weapon whilst another sat back basking in the sun. They seemed relaxed and peaceful, yet Yehooda was not fooled by the casual appearance they held. He was well aware of the dangers these men presented and the destruction they were capable of.

For a moment he reflected on the War Of Independence when his army was attacked from all fronts. He had thought, as many of his contemporaries did, that there would be a respite. A moment of peace with the Arab neighbours, when Israel became an Independent State and the first Prime Minister of Israel, David Ben Gurion, was elected. The respite never came; Israel's new borders were attacked from all sides. The Egyptians conquered Ashkelon and advanced from the South towards Ashdod. The Jordanian Army took the Old City in Jerusalem. The Syrian Army crossed the Jordan River from the North. The Lebanese Army took control of the Lower Galilee and the Iraqi Army took hold of most of Judea. There was no peace and no let-off. The war was greater, more intense and an enormous threat to the new Israeli Government and its people.

The determination to survive and keep their independence gave them the energy to ignore the pain of death and battle against all odds and secure their borders. The Arab nations were temporarily halted and made to retreat. The pictures of dying men were deeply engraved in Yehooda's mind and a constant reminder of the dangers that lurked in every direction.

Yehooda judged the distance of the camp as some 500 metres away. He signalled his men to go left and right, manoeuvring them in different positions for a more detailed surveillance.

***

On the lookout and high up on a rocky structure was posted one of the terrorists. His high position afforded him a good view of the surrounding area whilst at the same time offering him protection from being seen. He had sighted the Israeli soldiers from the moment they left the road and advanced by foot. He had signalled the imminent danger to his fellow compatriots who in turn were able to quickly prepare an ambush.

He spotted the Israelis spying on the camp and circling the area. They were depending on the few men who were positioned around the fire to act as though they were unaware of their presence.

The trap was set.

***

Yehooda's men continued to move in different directions and as they neared the camp the terrain was much rockier and more difficult to negotiate. They were forced to enter a narrow gorge, their safety endangered by the route they were taking and the advantage of surprise compromised. Yehooda quickly moved from one boulder to another taking care not to trip on the very rough surface. His men likewise negotiated their routes and created a cloud of dust at the rear as they slowly advanced. Their eyes darted from one cranny to the next, from one rock to another, in their constant gaze for signs of the enemy and a possibility of an ambush.

The explosion came without warning. Even the sight of a huge flash left little time for evasive action. Time had run out. The Israelis were doomed.

***

"Dr Goodman," the receptionist announced, just as Shoshana arrived at the hospital. "Doctor Slomo is looking for you in surgery, there's been another round of casualties."

"Thank you, I'll be with him in a few minutes," replied Shoshana as she raced down the hallway.

Having seen her daughter safely mount the bus and having held on to devoted thoughts of Yehooda, she was now ready for the gruelling hospital work that seemed to increase with every day. As a general surgeon in the busiest hospital, she was a member of a team of 20 responsible for the well-being and care of hundreds of wounded soldiers. Many arriving on her table were barely alive with twisted bodies, missing limbs and horrendous wounds of hanging flesh. They were the lucky ones as most did not make the hospital.

Scrubbed down and gowned, Shoshana stood over the first casualty. A wide gash to the leg exposed both the extensor muscle and thighbone. An x-ray revealed a fractured femur. She worked quickly and neatly, cleaning the wound, sewing back the torn muscles, correcting the bone structure and placing the limb into a Thomas Splint. The skin was sutured back into line and the patient removed to make way for the next case.

The second casualty arrived with his feet missing, his uniform still on, and covered in clotted blood at the end of the shins. A tourniquet was strapped round each thigh to prevent further blood loss. Again Shoshana worked quickly in determining the best surgical action. A needle into the vein provided a sample of blood for cross matching and for a line to be inserted and attached to a saline drip bag to flow into the body. The assistant helped by releasing the tourniquet tension every so often so as not to starve the lower areas of blood. Shoshana removed the bones of both shins at a point near the knees and designed good skin flaps to cover the stumps. The patient had lost an enormous amount of blood and Shoshana's surgical skills and safe hands gave him the greatest chance of survival.

The injuries were never simple and were a consequence of the powerful bombs used in war. The army was sending healthy men to battle and the battle was sending them to destruction.

A sudden disturbance pricked her ears. Her eyes glanced from the patient and for a moment the scene distracted her thoughts. Nurses were running in panic as another group of wounded soldiers was admitted, a group in a worse state than the previous and with greater need than seemed possible.

Her day would be long. Later she would be able to get word back for a minder to look after Sheba on her return from school.

The new influx of casualties were prioritized and placed in a queue before being transferred to a waiting surgeon. Shoshana signalled her readiness for the next patient.

On her table was placed a male soldier whose whole body seemed to have been engulfed in fire and embedded throughout with pieces of shrapnel, the result of a missile exploding very close. The face was covered by a mass of open wounds making any features impossible to recognize. Looking along the upper torso some ribs protruded from their cage, their ends snapped and looking like pointed daggers. The stomach carried a gash from one end to the other with part of the intestines bubbling out. The lower torso was in no better shape. Yet, even in this ghastly state his heart continued to live, barely beating and with his blood pressure dangerously low. This was certainly the worst injury Shoshana had witnessed from the many war victims to land on her table. This case required specialist work, skin grafting and face reconstruction.

"Do we know who he is?" enquired Shoshana.

"He's from the Special Unit, lost all his features from the explosion. They weren't able to identify him," replied an assistant.

"I want to see how the back appears," Shoshana announced to her colleagues. "Just ease him over." The assistants helped to roll the patient onto the side. Shoshana reached her hand to the middle of the back and began to feel the lumber vertebral spine.

"L1, L2, L3," she announced as she moved her fingers downwards, pausing at every joint to double check for damage. She suddenly froze, her wide eyes locked in a stare and her mind trying desperately to analyse the moment. Then came the silent scream, its sound held back from shock and realization.

The spasm hit her like a bull with sharp horns, numbing her muscles as she collapsed in a heap onto the floor. No amount of consolation and help from her colleagues could make her ignore what she had felt. That familiar birthmark, the mole, she would recognize it under any condition. Yehooda's dying body lay on her table. She was helpless.

She screamed again. This time her voice escaping and sounding like a French horn hitting the high notes: wailing, crying, weeping and howling. Her love was wrenched from her heart. The man who shared her life, her joy and her soul was gone. She was alone.

***

The funeral etched into their being as if branded by a hot iron. A father and husband snatched at his most precious moment, when they had just settled and sorted their future. Shoshana sat holding Sheba; both were crying with tears of dismay. They sat together for days not knowing which direction to take, not knowing what the future might hold. As far as they were concerned the end had come. They no longer had a reason to continue.

Days turned to weeks. They were resigned to being at home, away from school and work, away from their family and friends and away from the life they once knew and loved. They refused help, words of comfort, cooked meals and a helping hand from their neighbourly friends. Everything was declined as if they had reconciled to wasting away and losing the will to carry on.

They said very little to each other. Sheba constantly enquiring why her daddy had left her when she was so young and Shoshana asking herself again and again, why, with all her surgical training and the many lives she had saved, she could not help the man she loved. The wounds were so horrendous, the battle was lost before he had reached the hospital. The answers evaded her; it was impossible to reason no matter how much they tried.

"Sheba we must talk," Shoshana woke her daughter. The clock on the wall showed 3.00 a.m. "Sheba I need to talk to you," continued Shoshana gently prodding her daughter awake. Sheba was easily awakened; to her, sleep was a number of light naps with gaps of anguish and torture. Her father's memory repeatedly drummed in her mind as she cuddled next to him, played games and listened to his gentle voice reading good night stories and fairytales.

"Sheba, we must talk."

"Hi Mum, I wasn't sleeping. I was just thinking of Dad." The words faded from Sheba's mouth as again tears welled in her eyes and flooded down her cheeks. "Oh Mum, I miss him a lot."

"I know darling. He loved you so much. He will always be with you. In your heart and wherever you go his memory will be there to remind you of wonderful times. Believe me, he misses you too. He also wants to be with you and he wants you to carry on and live with his memory." Shoshana was struggling to hold her emotions together, to put on a brave face and to show her daughter that they had to be strong and that life had to continue. They must not waste the wonderful years that brought the three together. "Darling, we must be brave and that's why I want to talk to you about the future. We have to make the best of what we have, you and I together as one. We have to fight our way through this terrible tragedy and continue the journey your father would have wanted us to take. God knows he would not have wanted us to mope around. Dad wants us to be strong, lift our heads up and together find a peaceful future full of happiness and joy."

"Mum I love you so much." Sheba burst into tears again, grabbing her mother tightly round the neck and burying her face into her shoulders.

"Darling, let's have no more of that, let's be strong. Here, let me wipe those tears away." Shoshana used her handkerchief to clear Sheba's eyes. "From now on we're going to hold back those tears. We're going to show everyone that nothing can destroy the power that we hold. We're going to take Dad's memory wherever we go and he will experience with us whatever we do."

"Oh, yes Mum. Dad will always be with us." Sheba's face suddenly lit up at the realization that her dad had not completely disappeared.

"Sheba, what do you say to moving south? I've heard of a lovely kibbutz, recently formed not far from Eilat."

Raymond Ross

Chapter 4

Sam blinked his eyes, slowly opening them and feeling the sting of the sun. He crunched his face to make his eyes smaller and to allow less dazzling sun into his blue irises. The shape in front slowly coming to focus was Billy's body standing over him.

"How do you feel?" enquired Billy. "You've been in and out of consciousness over the last five days. I thought at one time I had lost you."

Sam's pupils gradually came into line and he was able to see a clearer picture. "What happened? I-er, feel a little dizzy, a little light and weak. Where are we and who are you?"

"Shhhh we don't want to be heard. One question at a time. I'm Billy. We have to be careful. The ship has been taken over by some bandits; the captain was shot and the crew made to jump overboard. They don't know we are here. We have to keep very quiet. Do you remember being locked up in the first hold with all that cotton? I felt the hatch lid banging and when I lifted it, out you popped," reflected Billy. "You were barely alive with all those cotton fibres stuck down your throat. You were choking and gasping for air and your body was so exhausted you flopped onto the deck like a rag doll. I dragged you over to the stern of the ship and we've been cooped up here for over five days."

Sam signalled he was thirsty. Billy tilted the mug, just as he had done so many times before trying to get liquid into the young lad. He had taken the food and water at night when the store was left unattended. After all, he knew his way around, every corner and nook. He could stay in the shadows and away from the threat of the bandits.

"Yes I remember now. I was running away from the Law. I was starving, there was no food at home and I took a roll from the bread man. He saw me and chased me down the road. I hid behind some bales and before I knew it I was hoisted up onto the ship." Sam stopped for another breath of air and another gulp of water, and then suddenly jerked backwards. "Are you one of the bandits?" he stammered.

"Oh, no," replied Billy, "I was with the crew. You saved my life. In fact we saved each other's lives. If you hadn't been trapped in the hold, I would have been caught and thrown overboard."

"Where are we heading?" enquired Sam.

"I'm not completely sure. I think we've been travelling in an easterly direction and by the change in the temperature I reckon we must be heading towards the Middle East."

Sam fell back to sleep, no doubt his body still having to contain its strength. Billy continued to watch over him.

***

"Land Ahoy," sounded the news. Billy was well awake and alert. There had been a lot of movement among the men on the deck and it seemed as though something was brewing.

"Sam, wake up," he whispered.

Sam stirred from his sleep, rubbed his eyes and looked more refreshed than the previous day.

"It looks as though the ship is about to reach Port. Welcome to Egypt," continued Billy in a humorous fashion. They both looked over to where the men had gathered. "Look they're opening the second hold."

The men were busy lifting boxes out of the hold and stacking them on the deck. "You see that European guy over there," whispered Billy, "I heard them call him O'Donnell. I believe he boarded the ship in Liverpool. He had that consignment loaded. Sam took a good look at O'Donnell. Somehow his features became ingrained in his memory, a mean looking man and Sam had that strange, sixth sense, feeling that somewhere in the far-off future he would turn up again.

O'Donnell used a crowbar to heave one of the boxes open. From inside he drew out a rifle fitted with a telescopic sight. Then he took another and another, tossing them to the men. They fondled the rifles and pretended to aim, playing with their new toys, bouncing them, loading and cocking them. Their broad smiles gave away their delight and joy of owning the new and powerful weapons.

One of the men pointed his rifle in the direction of Sam and Billy. He was concentrating on one of the strands of rope tied to the mast, feeling quite confident he could split the rope with a single shot. Slowly he tightened his grip, pulled the trigger a bare millimetre and stopped. He held the position for ages. Billy spotted him, held Sam down and dipped his own head out of view. The man's shooting eye spotted the movement. He stood rigid, in between two breaths, to consider the sight.

Lowering the rifle the man moved forward for a better view of what he thought was possibly an animal hiding behind the barrels. He walked over to them.

Sam and Billy moved further round and into the cover of the Lazerith area. The man was a little puzzled. Whatever he had seen seemed to have disappeared. He moved further forward taking care not to make a sound and checking that his boots only lightly touched the wooden floor of the deck. A single creak could give away his presence and frighten whatever was hiding ahead. Step by step he moved forward.

Sam and Billy slid further down their hide, they were nestled against the gearing wheels used to steer the rudder and the ship. The man entered the Lazerith, sweat dripping from his forehead, looking very menacing. The rifle now balanced in one hand whilst he used the other to support himself as he crept forward.

Billy signalled to Sam, whispering. "We mustn't be caught. We'll have to make a run for it. Are you ready?"

At the moment of tensing their muscles to sprint, the man turned and gave up looking. Relief quickly spread through their bodies as they relaxed from the prospect of being detected.

Remaining pressed against the gearing house for the rest of the day and deciding not to chance the daylight, they would wait for right moment before making any attempt to disembark. On the approach of nightfall the ship dropped anchor close to the shore. The time was right and Bill and Sam were not going to take any further chances of being detected. Securing a rope to some railings by the port side they slowly scaled down the side of the boat. Billy was well trained in rope climbing and scaling down heights in emergencies. To Sam, all was not so simple. He did not have the strength to support himself and, in spite of wrapping his legs round the rope for extra grip, his hands gave way. Half way down he lost his hold and plunged into the sea below, sinking from the force of the fall. Billy's alertness enabled him to surface dive at the right moment and secure a strong hold on Sam's shirt, thus preventing him from drowning. Sam bobbed onto the surface, spluttering and choking from the presence of water down his throat, and the two of them kicked furiously to keep afloat.

"Hold on to me!" screamed Billy. Sam grabbed Billy's strong arms and clung on to him whilst the two of them made their way to the shore.

With nightfall the temperature sank rapidly, the clear sky allowing the full moon to glow brightly. The shimmering water reflected the moon's presence and lit the way for the two youths.

At the side they climbed onto the sandy beach by the port house. A large painted sign informed them that they were in Port Said. Neither was any the wiser as to their whereabouts. Behind them were many fishing boats moored at the port, and in front a rough road winding towards what looked like an open market area. Laden trailers were being pulled by harnessed donkeys in both directions, bringing goods to and from the port.

Having decided to distance themselves from the port and from the danger of the authorities, they raced down the road and up to the few market stalls still showing their wares despite the darkening hours. A number of stalls displayed fruit, fish and meat whilst others had leather goods, clothing and materials.

Making their way to a truck parked next to one of the fruit stalls they decided to see if it could be used as a shelter and a place to rest and dry their wet clothing. The truck carried boxes of watermelons and by rearranging the boxes they were able to create a space large enough for the two of them to hide. They were both exhausted from the dramatic encounters on the ship and both needed time to recharge their energies.

"You know, that's twice you've saved my life," said Sam. "I can see I'm going to be for ever indebted to you."

"Oh, think nothing of it," replied Billy "It's just a normal day," he mused. "Who'd have thought I'd be in the back of nowhere, sitting in a truck surrounded by watermelons, thoroughly wet and exhausted."

"Well this 16 year old owes you his life and, believe me Billy, I'll never forget you for it and will always be there if you need me."

"Hey, don't be so serious. Anyone would have done the same and anyway, remember, I would have drowned with the rest of the crew, had I not been looking after you," continued Billy.

"What do you think we should do next? How are we ever going to get home?" Sam was now getting a little edgy as he though about being away from home, in a country he knew nothing about, with no food, no money and nowhere to go.

"Relax Sam," said Billy. "Don't get over anxious. Tomorrow we'll go to the police station and report the whole incident including what happened to you on the ship. No doubt they'll put us onto the next ship home."

Sitting down they relaxed and before long were in deep sleep.

***

The sudden jerk of the truck's suspension system startled the two of them awake. Dawn had arrived. They had slept the whole night and could no doubt have slept longer were it not for the lorry's engine coming to life. The lorry was on its way along a very rough road, bouncing along as it negotiated the many stones and rocks that lay loosely in its path.

"Billy are you awake? Where are we going?" Sam enquired, wedged between two crates and realizing the lorry was speeding forward.

Billy could only shake his head to indicate he had no idea as he bounced up and down from the motion of the lorry. Before long the crates shook loose and danced along the floor, bruising and scraping at the two of them. They both held their hands up to prevent their bodies being battered to pieces but the force was too great and their efforts too weak.

The truck came to a stop. There was a reprieve. The crates come to rest and the relentless bruising stopped. The driver hopped out of his cab and walked over to a café for breakfast. Billy looked around. In spite of being totally bruised and in a distressed state, his instinct warned him not to leave the truck at this place but to continue the ride until they reached a town where they could seek help. He also knew that they had to do something about the loose crates, even if the driver chose to ignore his

46

goods. The crates had to be secured. A number of other open trucks were parked by the café. Billy jumped off the truck and looked into those parked at the side and was able to find some loose rope and a couple of worn tyres. Fastening the crates together the two fashioned a hiding place for themselves and used the tyres for seats. They were determined that the rest of the journey would be both easier and safer. After having just finished their hide the driver reappeared, jumped onto his driving seat, turned over the motor and continued on his journey.

Billy and Sam, now a lot more comfortable looked back at the distant café, realizing they had not eaten for hours and suddenly feeling the hunger pains they had resisted for so long. They looked at the watermelons and then at each other. The signal was obvious; both had come to the same conclusion. They did not waste another minute. Lifting the lid off one of the crates they hurriedly took some melons out, cracked them against the floor and feasted on the goods.

The driver concentrated on the road ahead. This was his weekly trip from Port Said carrying fruit to some of the market areas that littered the length of the Gulf of Suez. Some weeks he would carry oranges and apples whilst on other weeks the load would be melons. The southern trip took him close to Cairo and as far as Danbarah. The journey stretched for many kilometres and the driving conditions were very tiring, especially in the midday sun when the temperatures would soar to well over 100oF. This day was no different from any other. He wiped the sweat off his face with the back of his sleeve, shuffled himself on his seat and tried to find a more comfortable position. He enjoyed his drink and was never alone without a bottle of whisky for company. When his throat was dry he would swig at the bottle just taking a little of the fluid, letting it slide down his gullet and tickle his insides. He was always careful not to overindulge only to find himself and the truck overturned at some nasty bend.

For several hours he continued the drive. The road often turned into a track, strewn with lumps of stones, some rounded and others with sharpened ends threatening to burst the thick tyres. The sand blew against the front and side windows of his cabin, obscuring his vision and irritating his eyes. He looked at the wing mirrors, they were covered with dust and offered no vision. Winding the side window down he reached over to the wing mirror to wipe the dust. That was when he spotted a green object being tossed out of the back of the truck.

"What the..?" he muttered to himself.

He looked again. Another green object flew from the side. This time he kept his eyes on the object as it hit the roadway. It was a piece of melon.

***

"Where are all those things going to go?" laughed Shoshana looking at her daughter's packing. "You can't take all that, we'll be moving into an apartment much smaller than this one. There just won't be any room."

Since deciding to leave Tel Aviv, Shoshana had struggled with sorting Yehooda's possessions: the sweet smell of his clothes, the soft fibres running through her fingers and arousing her feelings. The ties neatly hung on the rack just as he had always arranged them and there was the odd way he would leave his shoes with their laces tied when not worn. The feelings were just too strong for her and always ended with tears, with despair and hopelessness. She would never forgive herself for Yehooda's death.

Somehow Shoshana was able to hide her feeling of depression. She did not want to put any more stress on her daughter who had her own sadness over the loss of a father. Whenever Sheba confronted her, Shoshana would quickly pad her eyes dry and put on a broad smile to further hide her great sadness. She just had to provide broad shoulders to support her daughter and give her confidence for the future.

"Why don't you put your dresses and school clothes in the small case and then you'll have room for books and all those odds and ends you want to take in the larger case? We could put some items into storage and then when the time is right have them brought over. That would mean we wouldn't need to throw anything away."

"What about Dad's things?"

"Darling, don't worry," continued Shoshana before Sheba had time to think too deeply, "we can put Dad's things into these boxes, they can go into storage too. Here hold this small one high. You see when we want them," as she said the words she tickled Sheba under the armpits, "we'll just get the boxes back." She laughed as Sheba dropped her hands, letting the box fall on the floor and then also bursting into laughter.

The two of them continued to laugh and tickle each other as they rolled on the floor like little kids at a party. One minute Shoshana held Sheba down and the next she rolled over with Sheba on top blaring hilariously and tickling at the same time. On and on they rolled, laughing and screaming, screaming and laughing, the joys of a mother and daughter relationship deafening the house like two cheeky monkeys swinging on branches.

They were ready, the time was right. They would leave the old life and take the road to a new adventure, excitement and a new beginning. The truck would come for them at 8.30am the following day.

***

The boys had been busy tucking into the melons, resting between bites and even having the odd nap. The melons were so mouth-watering and delicious, they just could not resist them nor did they want to. They were quite happy being driven along, sitting on the bouncy cushioned tyres and without a care in the world.

The truck came to a stop at the side of the track. Sam looked back and saw the driver jump from his cab, his right hand waving a revolver and his left supporting a knife. The driver hurried to the side of the truck and on seeing the two lads cursed with a burst of Arabic. He raised his gun and frantically began firing in all directions.

"Jump!" shouted Sam.

The two jumped from the far side of the truck as bullets came flying at them. They ran with spinning feet, clambering up the loose sandy hillside of the track and then diving for cover. The driver's shaky aim followed, no doubt driven by the wobbly messages sent from his whisky soaked brain.

He had not the strength to chase them but just growled and cursed like an angry dog. Raising both hands in the air he carried on shooting until the revolver barrel was empty.

The two youths continued their run thinking the madman was still shooting at them. On they ran, down the other side of the hill, up the next and down again, frightened of looking back and too terrified to stop.

Their energy sapped and exhausted they both fell onto the stony sand, half burying themselves from the impact and with hearts racing to catch air into their lungs. Recovery was slow. There was no choice. They had to continue or face the possibility of being followed. Again they struggled to press ahead and to distance themselves from the track.

Time seemed to stand still. The sun blazed relentlessly from the open sky, not wanting to dip the horizon and give refuge to the two wanderers as slowly they trudged forward. The heat of the desert covered them like insulation. Their skin pores were unable to cope with the rising temperature as their body water reserves slowly dwindled through evaporation.

The awakening of dusk came not a moment too soon. The sun had finally given up on them and taken itself to another part of the world, allowing the exhausted two the pleasure of the cooler night.

Sleep came quickly and with it the opportunity to recharge in readiness for another blistering day in an oven like environment. The humidity soared in harmony with the temperature, both working together in a powerful way and inviting man and beast alike to their mercy.

The following day the two continued to defy the hardship that engulfed them with extra terrestrial energy, as if from another planet. Lost, confused and overwhelmed by the terrain encircling them, they travelled on without any idea of direction but somehow being pulled by some magnetic force, like a compass needle floating ahead, directing and pointing the way.

Relief came suddenly. As they climbed yet another rocky hill they saw a mirage floating in hot air like a magic carpet. At first looking suspiciously as if the desert had become an ocean. Their eyes took ages to focus on the delightful sight of a huge water expanse stretching from north to south.

Soon they were bathing in the cool water.

"Billy, can you see that boat ahead? Looks like a small fishing boat." Sam was right. When they looked more carefully they could see a number of boats bobbing on the surface. They all had long nets draped over the side. Men hauled their catches in and threw their nets out in a constant cycle.

A boat nearing them read 'Jezabel'. The boatman, busy with his catch, was drifting closer. They waved and waved, shouted, whistled and made all sorts of noises to be heard. Only when the boatman finished with his haul did he look up. He had noticed them and was on his way to pick them up.

***

The slow journey through the Negev, in a truck, bouncing along on uneven tracks, left Shoshana and Sheba totally exhausted. They had not experienced such a difficult terrain as the rocky desert stretching from Be'er Sheva to Eilat. Weary and fatigued they reached their destination, a small settlement of a few hundred inhabitants living together and breathing new life into the barren surroundings. They were in Eilot, a small kibbutz just a few kilometres from Eilat. This would be their new home, their new life and adventure.

***

"This is as far as I'm going. The boat journey ends here," announced the boatman aboard the 'Jezabel'. He had been their lifeline and saviour. He had given them new hope and had brought them to safety.

"Where are we?" enquired Sam.

"Eilat."

Fortune had entered their life when they sighted the boatman, a British citizen who, on Israel's Independence and departure of the British troops, decided to remain in the area he fell in love with.

Having picked up the two desperate lads his voyage took them south along the Gulf of Suez then north to the Gulf of Aqaba where the Red Sea ends at the southern most tip of Israel, at Eilat.

Chapter 5

"Hi. Can I help? Those bags look bloody heavy," enquired Jack.

Shoshana had not noticed the fair-haired young man. She was too busy organizing the cases out of the truck and making sure she did not lose sight of Sheba. She looked up. He was standing by a stack of rubbish, shovel in hand and sweat rolling down his cheeks.

"Thanks. I er, thanks I hope you don't mind. The heat's so fierce." She paused to wipe her brow. She was about to thank him again but there was no need, he did not need another cue. He did not give her a chance to utter another word. He was there pulling the remaining cases from the truck and hauling them into the apartment.

"I heard new visitors were coming. You were expected yesterday. Oh, I'm Jack." He pushed his hand forward to shake hers. She was about to take it when she saw the dirt.

"Er I'm Shoshana," she replied taking a step back and almost too embarrassed to talk.

"Oh, shit. It's the dirt." He spat at his hands and rubbed them together, wiping them on the side of his shorts. Again he put his hand forward. She froze looking at it. There was no way out. She had to take a grip and lightly held it as they shook. He looked at Sheba.

"Oh, this is Sheba, my daughter."

The rest of the cases and several boxes followed into the hallway.

"Been to a kibbutz before?" enquired Jack. "I suppose you know it's the Hebrew word for group, gathering together, a communal settlement. It's not like living in the big city. Here everyone works together. We're a single family; we look after each other and share our experiences. It only needs one of us to feel bad and everyone is affected. You'll see. Once you get to know everyone you'll feel the same."

Shoshana and Sheba quickly settled in their new home, their life slowing down a pace or two, giving them more time to relax and enjoy their daily experiences. There was rarely a day when they did not think of Yehooda and, although tears would frequently surface, the feeling of grief gradually settled, allowing them a little more laughter with every passing day.

Sheba attended the small school run by members of the kibbutz and became a very popular student. She had grown quickly and matured in stature to become an attractive and lovable member of the community. She was the eldest pupil in the small mixed school, whose age range was from six to fifteen. Those of the younger generation were housed in a dormitory close to the school area whilst their parents worked for the good of the kibbutz. The few older children were looked on as young adults and sent to the army to complete their service for the country. Sheba knew her place in the forces was drawing nearer and looked forward to the challenge and opportunity of proving to her father that his life was not wasted. She would carry his name forward. He would not be forgotten.

For the present she threw herself into every task given by the kibbutz members, never questioning or showing signs of being disgruntled. Her determination to succeed in whatever she did outpaced her rivals; often leaving them at their starting blocks before they realized the work was complete. Even at such a young age Sheba was able to pass her school knowledge to the younger children with the technique of an experienced teacher, showing by example how learning can be fun if approached in the right way. The kids took to her so easily and for the first time looked forward to their lessons.

Sheba's mind was made up. She would serve her term with the army before entering higher education for a teaching course. She eagerly anticipated the many years she would devote to the children of Israel.

Shoshana suffered greater pains from the scars caused by the loss of Yehooda. Hers were more deeply etched into her daily activities. She found him regularly appearing in her mind, his kind face and cheerful smile, the laughter that would send her senses into orbit and the solid love that united them. The nights were harder to bear as she lay in a lonely state. His knees no longer tucked under hers. His firm hands no longer embraced her, his manly smell now absent and no longer drifting through her sheets.

She ignored all thoughts of losing Sheba to the army and temporarily lived in a state of pretence, as if living a lie, not wanting to face the realities of her surroundings nor those of Sheba.

Alas the day came for Sheba to move on. The army beckoned. She had grown into a woman and was ready to take her part in the cause of the State of Israel. Shoshana was devastated as the jeep carried her daughter out of the gates, even her waving hands could not comfort her deep pains. In a moment her baby was gone. She was alone.

***

Sheba reported to one of the many basic training camps in the Negev for intense army training.

The next day Nasser sent Egyptian troops into Sinai to close the passage from the Red Sea to the Port of Eilat and, in spite of UN intervention war broke out between Israel on the one side and Egypt, Jordan and Syria on the other.

Israel Air Forces launched a pre-emptive strike on the Egyptian airfields. Their ground forces took control of the Gaza Strip and the Sinai Peninsula. The area of Judea and Samaria were captured to the west of the Jordan River and at the southern slopes of Mount Hermon the Golan Heights were conquered. The whole episode took six days in 1967 and in that time three Arab military forces had been defeated. The narrow stretch of land between Samaria and the sea was broadened and Jerusalem was reunited with its eastern half.

Sheba saw very little of the war and continued her intense training, covering all areas, from uniform management to fitness training and weaponry use. Women were not sent to the front lines, their work being centred round support, administration and materials' handling. These tasks included such important work as folding and preparing parachutes for the air force, operating communications and switchboards, manning radar monitors for analysis and interpreting aerial photographic shots. After basic training Sheba requested to join the teaching core where she could use her teaching skills to educate the many immigrants who were entering the forces. She taught basic Hebrew and Mathematics.

***

From the moment Sam and Billy had arrived at the shores of the Red Sea of Eilat, they were staggered and captivated by the vision of the glowing distant rocky mountains. They served as a boundary to its glistening waters, the sight altering with every foot the sun took to straddle the horizon. One moment the colours were crimsons and reds and then tanned yellows and browns. They were hypnotized by their glow and magnetized by their wonder. Night would bring a chill to the air, a glow of sparkling stars against the rippling waves, the sky always clear and allowing space to display itself in an ever-changing fashion. Then Dawn would show itself, its sun sending beams of light to announce the coming of a new day and paint the sky in shades of pale blue. Only rarely would there be a flutter of clouds in defiance of heaven. The place may have been barren, hot and dry but to them it was something new, something they had not experienced before, and something they knew they did not want to let go of.

Their priority was to find a piece of ground where they could find shelter, somewhere to sleep. They were introduced to the Town Office and informed that they could pick a small area to pitch a tent, away from the town and where there were no other dwellings.

"Just find a small space, away from this immediate area and let us know your choice and we'll record it as yours," the clerk recommended.

From a nearby army camp they were able to obtain canvass together with some provisions and trudged towards the deserted area adjoining the beach.

"I fancy just here, near the tree so that we can have shade," suggested Sam.

"No we'd be better over there, away from the beach. Over there about 100 metres away so that we don't get any disturbances from anyone roaming the beach," argued Billy.

"No the tree will be good for us," continued Sam

"But the beach could become busy," persisted Billy

The discussion of where they should camp continued for ages in spite of the fact that the whole area was desolate and they could have had the choice of many little spots.

They arrived back at the office and informed the clerk that they could not make up their minds. To which he laughed, "Well, why don't we record both spots and then you could decide later?

Sam won the day; they settled by the sea. Their home became a tent, spacious enough to accommodate living areas for the two and an ample area for storage. For their back yard they had the beach and for their view all the beauty their eyes could focus on. For cash, they scoured the small town for odd jobs, cleaning windows, brushing floors, mending broken wooden structures and doing whatever else they could turn their hands to. Where cash was not available they would settle for clothes and food.

The town area was yards from the beach, small and dusty, and had entered Israel's hands in 1949 after the War of Independence with some 500 settlers. A single road wound through the centre from which houses branched. Everything seemed to come in ones, a single store with food, a single café, and a single bank. There were no two businesses alike and the people worked in harmony in the belief of their land.

The growth of the port, the opening of the Timna Copper Mines and the expansion of the town caused a swell in the population with immigrants from North Africa, Rumania, Hungary, South America and with Israeli-born 'Sabras'.

Sam and Billy became familiar with the lay of the land and the daily movement of the town's people. It soon became quite apparent as to who did which job and where every item of necessity could be acquired. The idea of them working at the copper mines was the result of seeing daily trucks taking workers out of Eilat. On further investigation they learned of the lack of manpower at the mines and the lucrative incentives offered to those willing to toil in the heat of the desert. This was just the opportunity they were looking for, a way of earning money and setting themselves up in a country in which, as foreigners, they had to cope with the language and variety of cultures. As far as they were concerned any idea of returning to England was as remote as going to the moon. There was no way back, only forward, and the copper mines offered them that hope.

***

"Anyone at home?" He rapped at the doorknocker. "Hallo, Shoshana are you at home?" This time he turned the knob and slowly squeezed the door ajar. From the hallway he entered the apartment and found her in the lounge rocking on the easy chair, as it swung on its base.

"There you are, Shoshana for heavens sake are you alive?" She did not answer, just continued her endless rocking, tick-tock like her clock's second hand.

Her eyes pointed to a spot on the wall as if she was looking through the cement and focusing at a distant mirage. Her face was flat and straight as if frozen in time, a coma locking her mind totally oblivious to outside influences and hypnotized into depths of an unparalleled state.

"Shoshana," he called as his palms met in mid air with a slapping sound. Louder and louder he clapped in an effort to wake her from the dead and continued to call her name. Finally her pupils flinched. She half turned and looked at him.

"Jack." she stammered. "Sorry, I was in a dream"

"Are you OK?" he enquired. "We got a little worried you hadn't shown up at the canteen. Are you hungry?" he continued.

"Oh, I'm OK. I was just thinking about Sheba. I've lost Yehooda to the war and now it has taken Sheba from me." Tears rolled down her face. Jack knelt down holding her cheeks in his palms, the tears rolled onto his fingers and to his wrists.

"There, there, let it out, all that sorrow, all that grief. Just let it all out."

Shoshana dropped her head, her sadness so strong, her feelings in despair and her spirit broken. She just did not know which way to turn. Having settled in the kibbutz and joined in the daily routine work, she thought she

59

could hide from the depths of her heart but there was no relief. Her memories were too scarred by the past. Her only strand of comfort was there, holding her and absorbing her tears. Jack had been her right hand. Ever since the first day they arrived at the kibbutz he had been her guide, her friend. He had shown her the way of the kibbutz, introduced her to everyone and encouraged her to participate in its life. Now he was with her again, bringing her out of those black moments that haunted her saddened life. He guided her along, taking her slack hand, keeping it taut and reeled in, so as not to let her meander in and out of her misery.

"Shoshana, listen. You need to occupy your time with tasks. You need to be doing something all the time, something useful that will take your mind away from your dreadful memories and I know just the right tonic. Shoshana are you listening?"

She looked up, her red eyes glistening from the rays of light, her pretty face wrinkled from the constant barrage of sadness. She was ready to try anything that would pull her away from her thoughts.

"Listen," continued Jack, "there is a maternity hospital in Eilat. They want to expand the theatre work to minor operations."

Shoshana looked away. This was not quite what she thought Jack was going to say. She had wrenched herself from her love of medical work. The guilt that she could have done something to save Yehooda was the one force that sent her to a life hidden in a kibbutz community. She was not about to take the chance of throwing herself back into the source of her downfall.

"Shoshana, don't." he gently turned her face towards him, "this is a perfect opportunity to prove yourself. What you did at that operating table was more skilful than any other surgeon could have achieved. What happened was not your fault. The damage was done. It was the bomb that killed Yehooda, not you."

The following day Shoshana made an appointment to see Mr. Erick Cohen, Consultant Gynaecologist and Director of the Eilat Maternity

Hospital.

***

"Dr Goodman, welcome, please sit down. Dr Cohen will be with you in a few moments. He's just ending his morning rounds. Can I get you some coffee?" The dark haired assistant took great care to make Shoshana feel at ease. The vacancy for a general physician had been advertised for a number of months without success. Eilat was not exactly the number one destination for doctors who wanted to develop their skills. They did not want their families at the outer borders of Israel or the far away and barren areas of Eilat. Her boss had been very explicit in his instructions and she remembered every word as if it had been ingrained in her mind. He had told her, should Dr Goodman arrive before he finished the rounds, to make sure she looked after her and gave her a good impression of the hospital and did not discourage her.

Two coffees and two hours later, Shoshana had secured her appointment as general surgeon. The post was to begin immediately and at an attractive salary. Shoshana was delighted to be back among patients, enabling her to recharge her spirits and provide good medical attention to those who needed her skills.

The wards accommodated expectant mothers in different stages of pregnancy, some having spent many days there due to complications, whilst others were being rushed in at the last moment of cervical dilation and at the height of their contractions. They were the lucky ones, in and out in a couple of days, no problems and a beautiful child to take home. Shoshana spent some time looking after the expectant mothers who showed signs of requiring surgical procedures and where complications were looming. She shared her time with other patients, male and female of all ages, who required general surgery, of which organ complications were high on the list of sufferings.

Raymond Ross

Over the weeks and months that followed her work rate increased with greater demand placed in her hands. She relished the extra load and took it in her stride as if immune from pressure, from her past and her distant grief. She was a new person who devoured her task with total commitment, enjoyment and full thrust.

Patients had heard of her good work and what they called 'the miracle of her hands'. They queued for her attention and when referred to large town hospitals chose to remain in little Eilat, for her diagnosis and personal treatment. She was quickly establishing herself as an eminent member of the small southern community, accepted in all social circles and relied on heavily for advice and counselling.

***

Sam pulled the cart a few extra yards closer to the pit. A larger surface of rock had been gouged open by the constant hammering of the pickaxes, the sharp end biting into the Copper layer sandwiched below and picking the soft metal into loose pieces for removal. Men shovelled the find into the cart, as lump after lump filled the transporter. From here came the smelting and final extraction of the copper. Usually a big find was of some 50% copper rich nodules. This was the Timna Valley, mined for centuries and located in the southwestern Arava some 30 kilometres north of the Gulf of Eilat. The workmen lived locally in camps and worked long and arduous hours.

Sam and Billy worked well together and the bosses soon discovered keeping them together paid dividends in their productivity. United, they were more than a dynamic force. They were able to extract more than double the copper of any of the other workmen. They were a good team and were rewarded handsomely. Every lira earned was placed in a secret place by their tent and once a week they would count the coins.

"One day, perhaps when we're much older, we're going to use that money to better ourselves. This tent is only a stepping-stone. We've made it this far, and fate must have greater things in store for us. You'll see Billy," Sam would repeat the same story night after night. "You'll see Billy, our time will come."

For the next three years they toiled at their work, always defying the hard and dry land, carving themselves success and counting their achievements by the number of liras hidden. This now amounted to 483 liras and was growing with every weekly wage packet, a figure they knew from the continual act of counting, sorting and bundling. The time would soon come when they could look to other opportunities for work and betterment yet, at the moment, they found satisfaction from their labours. The language was a little more difficult to master but they were able to get along with simple every day phrases in the company of their work mates, and those who hung around the beach. Good vocabulary was not high on the list of necessities they sought after to achieve the new life they were eagerly carving for themselves.

This particular morning had started just like any other at 5.00 a.m., with dawn just appearing. The men gathered at the base of the mine to collect their equipment before resuming their backbreaking work at the rock face. The copper layer tempted them to hammer their way through its surface for removal and extraction. As they broke the rock formation they used wooden props to support the face from collapsing. The condition of the props had been well ingrained into every worker's safety check, to ensure they were in order. Even though they showed signs of wear, the damage had to be severe before the management would permit replacement. On this morning both Sam and Billy took a position at the mine entrance gathering the wooden support beams and placing them in height order, sorting the good from the bad and checking the extent of cracks and splinters they displayed. Some splinters were so huge they stuck out like rusted nails almost the size of tent pegs. The posts, numbering in the hundreds, were delivered to the mined area by small pulley trucks travelling on metal rails. These trucks were also used to carry other materials and equipment in and out of the mine, to the copper face and to various locations along the excavated seams where they were required for easing the miners' work.

The sun was at its 45-degree axis when the two youths stopped to take refreshments, a time prior to its reaching maximum height when temperatures would be too great for work to be done effectively. They sheltered by a pile of wooden props to gather their strength, refresh themselves with water and chew the sandwiches they had made earlier.

"Do you realize what this day represents? Our anniversary," announced Sam, his face engrained from the daily dust of the mines, his eyes gleaming at the thought of what the day represented as he lifted his cup. "To us, and to the next three years." he proclaimed, tapping Billy's cup in one measured swing, spilling some of the liquid and draining the rest down his dry throat. "Three years ago we landed at the foot of the Red Sea and just look at us now." They had become like brothers, caring for each other and experiencing their daily lives as one, united in every thing they did and everywhere they went. The 'brothers' were inseparable, a single unit building a base for a solid future and a solid life.

"Yes I can see us," Billy reflected, "at the end of the world, an uninhabited land, two years of hard labour, and great day was had by all!" He gaped a wide and mischievous grin across his face, "here, this will see us through." He pulled a bottle from the sack strapped to his back, spun the lid, propelled it off the top and sent it hovering to the ground. They both took turns with deep swallows, allowing the alcohol to filter down their throats as they yelled their delights.

"To the next three years," saluted Billy.

"And to the three years after that," toasted Sam.

***

Joshua Finestein grabbed the starting handle, rotating it in circular motions as the engine coughed to life sending black clouds of carbon out of the exhaust and into the dusty air. The five-tonne lorry shuddered to life from its resting place, its axle rotating from below in wait of the gearing wheels connecting and sending the heavy vehicle forward. Joshua mounted the driver's cabin placing himself onto the seat and behind the huge steering wheel with its outer circumference pressing deeply into his bloated stomach. His belly button peeped through the gap of his shirt, where once a button stood guard but now it was shredded with strands of cotton fibres trying to escape. His belly flopped over the wheel like a mass of jelly being squeezed out of its container and slobbering over the side. To Joshua, the lorry was like his child. He knew every dent and scratch etched into the body. He knew every screw, bolt and nut that fitted together to construct the giant vehicle and he knew the temperament of the engine parts that brought life to its mechanical make-up and made it operate.

Joshua had been driving lorries for the mining company for the past five years during which time he had witnessed many changes to equipment used, to the areas of mining and the workforce employed. His was the easy job. He just sat in the lorry whilst the men on the ground loaded and unloaded the goods. He simply drove the vehicle down the hill to the loading area and then up again for its removal. As long as he looked after his vehicle the company took no notice of the many hours he spent sitting around. Probably boredom was the main reason for his poor health, lack of exercise and constant eating binges throughout the day. Being overweight gave his heart the extra strain for blood circulation, which for the past three years brought him angina pains and dizzy spells, symptoms that he feared would bring instant dismissal from his job. He was not about to jeopardize his only means of income nor was he going to spoil the good relationship he enjoyed with his employers.

Releasing the hand break, his foot slowly allowed the clutch pedal to rise, rotating the engine more quickly and bringing the gears into operation. With the accelerator pedal pressed down the lorry began to move forward, bouncing on the loose and rocky track as it rolled along, swerving from side to side and barely missing the jagged rocks which lined the side of the track. The sun had ignited the driver's cabin into an oven choked with heat and lacking humidity, a condition of immense temperature only slightly relieved by the breeze blowing through the open window as onwards the vehicle drove.

Joshua's veins bulged from overheating, his blood temperature trying to stay in control, his skin pores releasing sweat onto its hot surface and his heart working overtime to pump fresh supplies. The strain was enormous. The task was almost impossible and the consequences of failure dire. His heart gave up, the artery rupturing from the dynamic forces as he felt a most excruciating pain race across his chest and along his arm. He slumped forward, his mind rejecting any thought of what was happening, his hand and foot losing their grip as the vehicle went out of control, free-wheeling down the slope and towards the opening of the mine.

***

"You know, I could lay here all day, taking in the sun and resting my eyes from the dry dust." Sam commented as he lay for a short respite from his labours.

"Well, don't get too used to the idea," replied Billy. "There's another stack of posts to sort out and we're rapidly running out of time."

The roar of the engine boomed down the track sending loose rocks flying in all directions, like a hurricane swirling out of control and ripping everything in its path. The two youths looked up, just as the thundering lorry came racing out from the blanket of sand created from its spinning tires, like a bull charging at the matador intent on total destruction. Billy was the first to leap to his feet and seeing the runaway truck heading directly to where they had been resting he dived at Sam, landing on top of his frame and pinning his face to the ground.

The impact of the truck as it struck the neatly stacked posts was like a bowling ball striking skittles and sending them crashing in all directions. The posts flew like darts, hurling themselves wherever they could cause the biggest impact and the greatest damage. Nothing was protected from their force; everything was mowed down, smothered and flattened.

The truck continued its rage before bouncing off a solid rock face, rolling over in cartwheels and finally coming to rest at the bottom of the track where it exploded into a fireball. The driver incinerated into ash and the lorry twisted into rubble beyond any recognition of ever having resembled a moving machine.

After the catastrophic storm, came a moment of tranquility. The ghostly dust settled into the silence. There was no sound, only stillness, not a movement. Even the breeze had been shocked by the sudden and powerful forces it had witnessed.

Before long several miners appeared from within the mineshaft who, having heard the explosion, raced to see if they could offer any assistance. The reality of the disaster and devastation was blinding their vision and appeared too harrowing for their lenses to maintain their focus. A small hand peeking through one little gap and a foot through another were the only signs to indicate the whereabouts of Sam and Billy, crushed and buried from a moment of driving madness.

The men pulled and pushed at the posts, tearing at their muscles and roughing their skins with splinters as moving post after post opened a clearer view of the two. Billy was lying above Sam, the two sandwiched between posts and both barely alive, clinging by the faintest of heartbeats. At the side of Sam lay a post, fastened tightly against his body with its tent peg lodged and well anchored, the blood dripping at the edges in readiness to burst and empty his life. Another post had lodged itself against Billy's head and having smashed his skull was threatening to pierce his brain tissues should the men disturb it from its resting place.

***

News of the accident was conveyed to Eilat Hospital. The medical team prepared themselves for the two casualties, making room for possibly two surgical procedures and sorting the required instruments. From the information given to Shoshana, the type of injuries described would have prompted her to divert the emergency to the main hospital in Tel Aviv where they were better equipped to deal with more complicated and extensive trauma cases. However, the emergency was of such a nature, she did not believe the two would make the lengthy journey alive. They needed immediate attention and, in spite of the hospital's sparse facilities there was no alternative. She would have to operate on the two; their lives would lie balanced in her hands and their future in her reactions.

Sam and Billy were carefully lowered off the two vehicles used to ferry them down to Eilat. The task of moving the wooden posts from their bodies had been an enormous problem and a major reason for the delay in them reaching the hospital. The first aider based at the mine had little experience of such an incident and could offer very little medical help. He managed to stem the flow of blood from Billy's head wounds but was unable to stop the seeping of blood from the edges of the peg embedded into Sam's body.

The two were placed on trolleys and pushed into the building where Shoshana placed herself in readiness for their arrival. With stethoscope in hand she examined Sam first.

"Get him straight into the theatre, he's losing blood, BP's down and he's about to go into shock." Then she turned her attention to Billy. There was no pulse. She shone a finger-torch at his eyes. They were fully dilated and still. "Get this one to Dr Cohen, then quickly follow me." The instructions came fast and precise. Time was precious and she did not want two fatalities.

Sam was placed in theatre as Shoshana rushed to his aid. He was put on a drip of insulin and assessed for injuries, the most prominent of which was the peg sticking out of his midriff, just below the belly and to the side. With her expert skills, Shoshana made a single incision across the abdomen to give her plenty of room to manoeuvre the peg from its hold. The abdomen was filled with blood, spilled from ruptured vessels. This would be removed by suction and only then could the damage be fully assessed.

***

"Wake up Sam." Shoshana called tapping at the back of his hand. "Wake up, wake up." Sam stirred from his sleep, moaned a little and dozed off again. "He'll be fine now," Shoshana informed the nurse and requested she check him every half hour. "Please let me know the moment he is fully awake," and with that she was gone.

For another eight hours Sam floated in and out of consciousness, never quite aware of his surroundings but knowing that every time he attempted to turn or move there was a sharp pain deep in his stomach and back. As he slipped back to sleep the sight of bobbing waves would appear in his mind as they splashed against the side of the ship, spraying their foam contents over the surface like soap bubbles out of a bath. The waves were seesawing with the rhythm of the tide, the magic of the sea swirling and shimmering, and in the distance a small head afloat, wading to keep atop and in view. The head up and down, the mouth wide-open shouting and screaming until it disappears.

"It's Billy, it's Billy. Someone help Billy, help Billy." His words disturbed the ward. "Where's Billy, where's Billy?" Sam continued as he came out of his sleep.

"Keep still, try not to move." advised the nurse. "You don't want to tear at the stitches," she continued, holding him firmly so as not to damage his dressings.

"Where's Billy?" Sam would not relent. He had seen his friend in his dream, he had seen him struggling for breath and going down. "Where's Billy?"

"Keep still, I'll get the doctor." As the nurse disappeared Sam darted his eyes in all directions trying to take in and understand where he was and why he was in a strange bed, the sores biting into him every time he attempted to move. As he looked down he could see bandages wrapped round his stomach. A tube protruded from his body and leaked fluid into a swab. Wires from his upper body were fastened to a monitor with lights blinking. The sight was almost overwhelming, too much to take in, whilst at the tip of his tongue was rooted the question. Where was his friend and why was he not with him?

"Sam, I'm Dr Goodman," Shoshana spoke the moment she arrived at his bedside. "You're a very lucky young man and at the moment, you probably won't be aware of what happened. There was a bad accident at the copper mine when a runaway truck ploughed through a stack of wooden posts. One of the posts landed on you and lodged a protruding splinter, the size of a peg, into your abdomen." As she said the words she held her hands apart to indicate the length of the peg and impress on him the enormous danger it created. "The peg was lodged from the front and as far as the back of your abdomen," she continued, still using her hands to explain as she went along. "On entry, it had pierced your spleen, scraped across an artery, fortunately without causing a rupture, and then through your bowel before appearing out of your lower back. I removed the spleen, which is OK; you can manage to live without one. I then repaired the bowel. You may find the trauma a little distressing and there may be some discomfort to begin with but luckily there should be no lasting problems. As I said you're very lucky to survive such a difficult operation."

Sam had a lot to absorb. So much had happened to him and he could not recollect everything. He tried to remember the truck, the posts and the accident but it just was not there. His mind concealed the information as if it did not want him to know the details.

"Where's Billy, where's Billy?" Sam persisted in his asking whilst pushing his problems to the back of his enquiry list.

"Billy?" questioned Shoshana. "Oh, you mean the other injured person brought in at the same time. He wasn't as lucky, landing on top; he may have prevented other posts hitting you. Unfortunately he suffered extensive damage to his skull from a post smashing his head. We did everything we could but he died."

Chapter 6

The news of Billy's death smashed into Sam's fragile body like a hammer through glass, shattering his thoughts into tiny fragments and scattering them throughout his nervous system. His voice was stunned to silence with its latent scream stuck at the back of his throat, his eyes blocking the daylight in a fixed stare of panic with eyelids glued back and eyelashes standing rigid.

Shoshana had not expected such a response and was not prepared for the sudden shock that accelerated through Sam. It had taken her by complete surprise. Even her medical training failed to guard her against the reaction. She had totally misread the situation and was contemplating the next move when he stirred from his trance. He looked at her questioningly.

"I'm sorry, Sam," she stumbled, "I didn't know Billy meant so much to you, I er, thought you were merely working together. How well did you know him?"

Sam related the story of their meeting in the middle of the Atlantic and how Billy had saved his life, looking after him. He told of their arrival at the shores of the Red Sea and everything that had led them to work at the copper mine.

"Billy was like a brother to me," continued Sam. "In fact he was the only person I really knew. Now he's gone, there's no one, nobody I can call a friend and nobody I can turn to for advice and help. We did everything together, looked after each other, shared the single tent on the beach and cooked for each other. I just don't see how I can continue without him." As he spoke, tears trickled down his cheek, with the sincere words of the feelings he shared with his best mate, now no longer with him and gone forever.

Shoshana instantly saw a mirror image of the experience Sam had related, to that of the suffering she had experienced over the last few years, ever since she had lost Yehooda and the effect his death had had on herself and Sheba.

"I'm so sorry Sam, for not appreciating the circumstances of your relationship with Billy. I can see now, it was wrong of me to have given you the news in such a heartless way. Do forgive me."

"You know, I have a daughter called Sheba. She's about your age, at the moment in the army but I hope to have her back in a few months. Her best friend was her father, they shared many wonderful years. We both love and miss him so much since he was tragically taken away from us, snatched at the height of our wonderful life, when we were really settled and felt that everything was going our way. His sudden death left us hollow and desperate, not knowing which way to turn. We were lost. We spent months feeling sorry for ourselves; we went through a terrible time of not talking to or seeing anyone. We just spent our days in isolation and cooped up between four walls, not wanting to move, go anywhere, do anything. We just existed." As she said the words she bowed her head, not able to keep her eyes fixed on Sam, feeling the pain of her words and the tragic memory she so wanted to forget.

"Sam, you mustn't let yourself be affected by what has happened to Billy. You've got to be tough and live your life to the full, in memory of your wonderful friend who'll always be with you in your mind and with whom you'll be able to share all your life's experiences. You'll see, just as I think of Yehooda whenever I have a problem or when I arrive at a new turning I always say to myself, "What would Yehooda do? Which way would he go?" You'll see. You'll do the same. Your friend will always be there and together you'll achieve everything you set your mind to."

Shoshana clasped Sam's hand in both of hers, in an endeavour to calm his thoughts and let him reach for her help. If she could release some of the grief and distress that had invaded his world he would have a better chance of being positive and moving forward.

***

Three weeks later Sam was discharged from the hospital, his mind made up not to return to the copper mines. He was putting his past aside and heading for a new future. The idea had come to him whilst he was recovering in hospital, from days of having little to do and from the boredom of the ward.

With the money Billy and he had saved Sam was scheming to convert his living accommodation into a refreshment bar by the beach where the young could gather at night and at weekends, let their hair down and enjoy a relaxed and laid-back atmosphere. He commissioned a carpenter, purchased all the necessary building materials from a local store and set about creating the perfect bar. There was standing area for about fifty people, a long bar at one end from where drinks and food could be served, a small sitting area and a room at the back which was to be his living area. This had a bed, kitchen and living room, all in one so as to allow as much space as possible for guests.

Two months from knocking in the first nail, the bar was completed, together with a big sign across the roof 'Billy's Bar'. Sam would always carry Billy's name, wherever he went and whatever he did. He would not be alone, his friend's spirit would always be with him.

***

The bar attracted business from the moment the doors opened. The young had always spent their free time by the beach and this was an opportunity to have a place to meet and have fun. The atmosphere became electric as the young adults of Eilat descended nightly to the bar, their guitars and violins adding an extra dimension to the enjoyment that blanketed the area. Not content with just being in the bar, they would spread themselves outside and along the beach.

Soon Sam had to cater an area of a 100metre radius from the bar. He employed a couple of hippies, Mary and June, to cover the outside area. They walked around, took orders, collected empty plates and glasses, and collected the charges. For wages, they would keep 10% and hand the remainder to Sam. Mary was the slimmer of the two, with long slender legs half hidden by a pair of flowered long shorts which had been full length before she scissored them down in size. On top she wore a baggy shirt with two fastened buttons and three loose, revealing her shapely breasts which supported rows of coloured beads looped round her neck and down her back. Her blond hair was combed straight and swept over her shoulders. June was different, tubby, dark and less attractive. In fact, customers would see the two as Jekyll and Hyde as if they were one and yet completely different.

One evening Sam was sorting out his stock and counting his weekly takings and whichever way he looked at the figures they just did not seem to add up. From the number of empty crates stacked at the back of the bar there should have been a greater return of liras. It was a simple sum that would not add up. One hundred bottles went out at 10 agorot each making a total of 1000 agorot, which is equivalent to 10 Israeli liras, and yet he could only count 5 liras. It was as if he were supplying drinks at half price and well below the price he paid. The following day he took more notice of the bottles as they left the bar, opened and served by the two hippies. He sold 60 bottles in all and when the girls brought the money they handed 3 liras.

"I'm a little confused," Sam began as he confronted the two girls, "this evening you served 60 bottles which should come to 6 liras and yet you only came back with 3 liras. Care to tell me about the balance?"

The girls looked surprised, they had not expected to be questioned on the matter and immediately became defensive.

"You must be mistaken Sam. We only served 30 bottles. There you are, see there's the 3 liras."

"I don't think so, there should be another 3 liras. Now would you mind telling me what you've done with the rest of the money, not to mention the money you've been stealing the past few weeks?"

With that comment, Mary ripped off her apron, threw the tray to the floor and stomped out.

"How dare you accuse us of stealing, you can keep the bloody job, didn't like it anyway."

Just as June was about to follow her out, Sam noticed a bag tucked under her side and fastened with a cord round her shoulders. His hand shot forward, grabbed the bag and tore it from her.

"Not with this, you don't."

She fled out of the bar. Sam took out the missing money from the bag and put it into his till, the girls were gone. He would never make the same mistake again. Learn from the past and conquer the future was his way forward.

The following day Sam employed Hamdy and Magda Vishara, a young and recently married couple from Egypt, who, having arrived at Eilat, made themselves known to a number of the local bars as seeking employment. They showed great knowledge of the trade. They had been a little hesitant to accept work from Sam, thinking a bar on the beach had little chance of survival, but Sam's gentle persuasion and enticement of good pay was enough to attract them.

From the moment the Vishara's began employment, the atmosphere round the bar became charged with an extra dose of ions, as if a new magnet had been installed to entice a greater grip of flavour. Hamdy's skilful and unique style of mixing drink concoctions transformed popular drinks such as Nesher Beer and Gazuz into new and exciting tastes whilst Magda's magic style of cooking brought humus, falafel, pitta bread, salad, corn and other titillating foods to the menu. At low costs, locals enjoyed an evening snack at the shores of the Red Sea, tickling their throats with spirited drinks, soothing their taste buds with seasons of the Middle East and sitting back and absorbing the panoramic views.

The benefits of Hamdy and Magda's contribution to the bar were reflected by the gradual increase in customer numbers, so much so that Sam's takings had risen dramatically and were hitting new records every week. Their relationship gathered momentum with every passing month and cemented concrete pillars, strong enough to withstand any weathering. They were a good team, united in their search for perfection and excellence, always wanting to please the customers and forever searching new heights of brilliance.

"Hamdy," Sam reflected one day as they took rest in the shade from the prevailing afternoon business, a rest, craved for by their muscles and pined for by their ailing bones. This was a respite they were forever searching for and having to forgo, in the name of keeping a busy bar popular.

"Hamdy," Sam continued. "You know you and Magda are very close to me. We work together like a family and I have grown very fond of your friendship."

"Ah, think nothing of it," Hamdy chuckled, "we are very grateful to you for giving us trust and allowing us to be part of the bar."

"Well today is very special. I'm 21, a birthday I should be celebrating with my family but as you are my family today, you can help me celebrate," Sam retorted laughingly, enjoying the thought of what might be happening this moment in Liverpool. He reached out for a bottle of lager, clipped the cap off and poured two glasses. "Here, L'Chayim and cheers to you, Magda and myself on my reaching 21" They swigged their drinks in unison, emptying the contents in one go and then raising their arms with a loud hooray. Both Sam and Hamdy broke into laughter in enjoyment of the moment.

"This place is heaven," shouted Sam, then turning to Hamdy continued in a powerful voice. "One day these shores are going to shine their presence throughout the world. Everyone will want to witness its magic, see its beauty and experience its splendour. They'll come from miles around, from all corners of the Earth. They'll bring their children, their loved ones, their families and they'll holiday right here where we are sitting. Can you imagine it?" Sam stood up and swept his outstretched arm in a semi circular arc, across from the hills bordering with Jordan to those bordering with Egypt.

"This tip, the southernmost spot of Israel, will one day be a place of great desire. They'll build hotels and restaurants along these shores. People will come and holiday here, swim in this very sea and relax on this very beach."

"Dreams, you mystify me with your dreams," Hamdy looked up at the sky. "There's your dream, up there floating like clouds," mused Hamdy. "You with such imagination, your head in the clouds. Ha!" he exclaimed, waving his hands as if trying to rid Sam of his nonsense ideas.

"It'll happen, you'll see and we'll be right here in the middle, 'Billy's Bar' in lights, serving the world with flavours of the Middle East." Sam was not going to be put off so easily. Billy had brought him to this land and with his spirit Sam was going to make great his name.

***

Shoshana enjoyed Saturdays, a religious day for the Jews, a day of rest and prayer and although she was an orthodox Jew by birth, she did not observe many of the laws and rituals. She had her standards and parameters with which she felt comfortable and was able to accept. As a child, life had been very different. She was brought up in a strict environment, a family steeped in Hassidic Jewish beliefs, taken to the extreme and followed to the absolute rule. Shabbat, symbolised the day of rest and engrained her mind with the many forbidden rules. Practices, which on weekdays were taken for granted and on this day were frowned upon. Her father was a prominent and well-respected member of the movement and by profession a scribe who excelled in the art of applying the tip of a feathered quill to parchment and scribing the words of the torah, the five books of Moses. It was a way of life for Shoshana, full of traditional values and well-accepted.

The first signs of Shoshana's meandering from the absolute religion appeared at medical school where her moulded beliefs were gradually chipped by the influence of other students. The care she felt as she gradually came in contact with patients from different cultured backgrounds, different beliefs and upbringings, demonstrated to her the similarity that existed when in hospital. They all experienced suffering, needed attention and endured their grief, their pain and stresses in the same way.

The telegram had dropped through her door some two weeks ago. 'Arriving home Monday 21st, love Sheba'. Her daughter was finally coming home, her army career over. They would be united and time could once again resume its normal place. She longed for Sheba to be home, to be with her sharing her daily tribulations, her joys, her mood swings, and best of all her company.

"Mum, I'm home". The door burst open to the living room, Sheba ran in and as the two embraced there was an instant explosion of relief. They were together again; no one would ever split them apart. They were as one.

The next few weeks were the best for Shoshana and Sheba, as they breathlessly recollected the last few years and attempted to bring reality to their experiences. Sheba told of her years in the army, the rigorous training she had endure,

Sheba's choice was to enlist into the elite Parachute Regiment which, being dominated by male soldiers, made her task more daunting. However her application was not put forward for recommendation by her seniors and she was assigned to a general posting.

She had cemented a close relationship with her fellow army recruits which helped to ease the constant face of terror and death of the relentless border skirmishes.

Shoshana in her turn described the hospital, her work colleagues and the patients, her happy life in the kibbutz and the many neighbours she had befriended.

"So, come on you haven't told me anything about Jack. Does he still come to your rescue?" giggled Sheba.

"Mind your own," winked Shoshana as she shifted uneasily on her chair.

"Well go on," persisted Sheba, "go on mum. From what I remember handsome, fair hair, blue eyes and anyway why haven't I seen him during these last few days?" She was not going to give up.

"He's away, a few fact-finding days for the kibbutz in Tel Aviv, something about flower cultivating and exporting. The kibbutz wants to develop extra areas of revenue," replied Shoshana in an attempt to change the subject.

"And…?"

"And, what?"

"Oh he's just a friend," explained Shoshana. "There's nothing more to it...." Her words trailed off as the front door flew open and from the hallway echoed the words, "Shoshana, I'm back."

Jack entered, flowers in hand and a broad smile to face.

"Hi, how have you been? Here I got you these, specially cultivated, their.." Jack stopped in mid sentence. "I can't believe. It's Sheba. My, look how you've grown, where's the teenager I eyed a few years ago?" Jack in turn reached over to Sheba, kissed her cheek and then focused on Shoshana.

Sheba was a little shocked and somewhat pleased by the sudden alertness of her mother's face, like a sunflower displaying its petals, her face glowing as she greeted Jack. Sheba viewed a reflection from the past, the way her mother and father had bathed in their warmth and joy, the way they talked and laughed and the way they had looked at each other. The same picture appeared in the room, memories of time gone by, of happy days, peaceful thoughts and joyous moments.

'Where did the last four years go?' she muttered to herself. Oh she was so happy; she was so pleased to see the youthfulness ecstasy brought back to her mother.

"It's time I went to shower." Sheba knew to make a quick exit. "So. There's nothing more to it!" She smiled to her mother as she exited.

***

"Can I help you?" Sam turned to the next person leaning against the bar. "Food or drink?" he continued. There was no response. "Are you next, can I help you?"

"Oh, yes I'm sorry. I was waiting for a friend. A lager please."

"Sure, coming up." Hamdy had taught him well. Sam expertly swung the bottle against the opener, flipped the top off and in the same momentum poured the contents into the glass without a single spill.

"There you go," Sam happily placed the glass onto the bar. "Ten agorot please," he continued. No response "The lager is ten agorot," he repeated." No response. "Are you alright?" Sam leaned over concerned his customer was not well. "Your drink," Sam pointed to the glass.

"Oh, thank you." The money handed over, there seemed no reason for Sam to remain attending to the same customer. Yet, he tried to move on but something held him back. He was transfixed, his eyes frozen in focus and his muscles pinned rigid.

"My friend should be here in a few minutes. Thank you for the drink." The customer's eyes locked onto Sam's. "Sorry, I, er didn't mean to stare. I'll go and wait for my friend outside." Now it was the customer who found it impossible to move.

Both pairs of eyes were gripped tight as if by an invisible chain whose metal links were fused together for life. They were momentarily oblivious to what ever else may have taken place in the bar. Sam yanked his head backwards.

"No, its me who's staring," he managed to utter as he swivelled his gaze to another focal point so as not to risk going through the same foolish incident.

"Who's next?" Sam hurriedly resumed his duty at the bar. A group of rowdy soldiers entered, pushing their way to the front.

"Hey, a drink," called out one of the soldiers. "Hey, a drink I said."

Sam looked up. They had placed themselves in the way of the customer and were pushing and shoving their presence.

"Do you mind?" retorted Sam in a harsh and firm way, then turning to the customer at the end apologised for the soldiers' behaviour. "Would you mind moving yourselves to the other end of the bar where I would be very pleased to serve, but we do have other customers to consider and I must ask you not to be so rowdy." With that, the soldiers moved aside. Sam turned to the customer.

"Sorry about that. Are you sure you're OK?" He was now a little concerned. She looked up at him and again he found himself transfixed by her beauty, her looks and her charm. "You say you're waiting for a friend."

"Hey, can we have some drinks down here?" Again the soldiers displayed their rowdy behaviour. Sam turned his attention their way thinking he had better serve them before there was any trouble. Two beers, three lagers and a couple of spirited shorts later Sam looked up to the girl at the far end. She was gone.

Chapter 7

The invasion came as a complete surprise, with the whole country at rest, no public transport, no radio or television and with most of the population fasting and at prayer. The day was Yom Kippur 1973, the most important day in the Jewish calendar and the day the Egyptian President, Anwar Sadat, commanded his army to attack Israel.

Thousands of soldiers were driven directly to the front lines from the synagogues to face the onslaught of the Egyptian and Syrian armies. Many Israeli soldiers were killed on duty during the first days of the war and many were taken as prisoner on both fronts. The Israeli Defence Force was able to recover from the surprise attack and reform to force the invaders into retreat.

Tank and paratroop forces crossed the Suez Canal into Egypt and came within sight of Cairo, surrounding the Egyptian troops and forcing them to surrender. In the Northern town of Ma'alot the Israeli Forces rescued children who were held hostage by terrorists.

The invasion had been sudden and the response quick. The result was a cease-fire agreement initiated by the American Secretary of State, Henry Kissinger.

***

The peace agreement gave some respite and offered a period of stability, even though it was not with all terrorist groups who regularly brought their own kind of terror across the borders. With peace came development, increased manufacturing and growth in the economy, the spin-offs reaching as far south as Eilat. The port of Eilat handled larger shipments and general trading in world commodities increased many fold.

Sam was prepared for change. He was ready for the influx of visitors and poised to expand with the demand. However, he did not want to change the concept of the bar he wanted to maintain the happy and friendly atmosphere it had developed and continue providing the specialised cooking his clientele enjoyed.

"Very soon we will have visitors from many different countries," Sam contemplated with Hamdy and Magda one late evening when the regulars had departed and only a few of the younger generation remained. "We will need to prepare ourselves to cater for a wide conglomeration of cultures and taste habits. There will be those looking for Oriental, Eastern, Mediterranean and European food, to mention but a few."

"But Sam, Magda and I are only familiar with our culture. How will we manage with others?" Hamdy responded

"We could employ other cooks and bar people as experts in their particular culture. In fact we could extend the bar in different directions." Sam could see all sorts of ideas coming into focus, his mind picturing Billy's Bar as catering for every taste bud that would ever walk through his doors. "Yes, we could have a central bar area from where small units of eating areas, each creating their own style of aroma, could be extended outwards. We could even decorate the individual areas in the style of their culture." The pictures were now developing quickly in his mind. "We could have an Israeli area, Arabian, Chinese, Mexican, Italian, Spanish. We could build the bar in the shape of a circle where there would be separate entrances for each area from the outside." The ideas just continued to flow. "It could be the shape of an octagon."

Sam was just too excited about the whole concept. Then he saw her again from the window. She was sitting by the beach. He stopped. Magda wondered what was wrong. Had he suffered a mental breakdown from all those sudden ideas? Was he going mad? She looked at Hamdy and could tell that he had similar thoughts.

"Sam are you OK? Sam." There was no reply. Again Magda asked the question. "Sam are you OK?" Hamdy and Magda sat, speechless in wonderment and shrugging their shoulders in question.

"I'll be back in a moment." Sam was gone.

"Hi, remember me, I tried to serve you a drink the other night," Sam stumbled along. "You were, er, waiting for a friend. The next time I looked up you were gone."

She looked up. The feeling from the previous encounter had flooded back as the tide does from the moon's magnetism, except in this instance it was not the moon but the barman leaning over her. He was tall and lean with long roughage of blond hair covering the back of his neck and almost to his shoulders. His fringe, like silken threads were loosely sloping over his forehead with some strands nestling against his thick eyebrows. His bright blue eyes were encircled by long swooping lashes. She was spellbound by his striking face, his cute nose, chiselled chin and soft lips. But it was his radiant and inviting smile that heightened her desire to stare at him unreservedly.

"Hallo. I said you looked as though you were waiting for a friend," Sam persisted.

"Oh yes, it was Janice. I'd met her in the forces. She was coming to Eilat to see me and some other friends. She'd not been here before and asked me to help her. Well I'm the person she felt most close to and she was confident being with and..." Then she realised she was rambling on with rubbish. Why should this barman want to know about her friend Janice? "Sorry, I er didn't mean to go on."

"Oh, it's quite all right. Please don't stop. Your friend sounds very interesting. Tell me more." Sam did not want her to stop talking. If she did she might think it was time to go and he certainly did not want to lose her again. "So did she enjoy Eilat?" Sam pressed on.

"You're just being kind," she continued as her eyes darted from left to right and back again like a clock pendulum. She was scared that if she stopped to look at the barman the clock would stop and he would be gone. "Janice loved the place. I took her into town. We went along the coastal road. We took a jeep into the hills. She met her friends. We went shopping then into a bar for drinks..."

"Slow down," Sam broke into a smile. "Tell me about yourself"

Only then did she look directly into Sam's blue eyes. The two of them were staring at each other, transfixed for ages in a cocoon of pleasure. Lost to the outside world and insulated from its activity.

"Sorry I didn't mean to stare." She pulled away for a moment.

Sam sat down. He wanted so much to know everything about the girl who was sitting at his bar. Her face was so beautiful, a beauty he had never witnessed at any other time. He was infatuated by her long bronzed hair, her bright blue eyes, full lips, small rounded nose, flat curved ears and slightly concave cheeks. Her skin looked pure and soft. He longed to touch her, longed to be with her, be part of her life. She was fun; she was laughter and joy all in one.

"What about now. Are you also waiting for a friend?" he enquired.

"No, I teach at the local school. It's my break, I usually come here for a drink," she replied

"Please let me get you something to eat," Sam wanted so much to please her, "some salad and falafel with pitta bread."

"No, that's very kind of you. I usually have a sandwich at school. I'm not really hungry."

Then Sam noticed Hamdy "I insist. Hamdy," he called over, "can the lady have an Israeli Salad please?"

She raised her hands to stop Sam from placing the order but was too late. The salad was placed at her table and she did not want to disappoint the barman sitting at her side.

"Here let me help you," Sam was so desperate to help her. "Pitta bread, Madam," he winked. "With diced salad, tomatoes cucumber and lettuce, a dab of hummus and of course, a couple of falafels. Made, may I say, with the secret ingredients passed down from Hamdy's great-great-grandparents." Sam continued to joke as he filled the pitta bread. "I hasten to add, Hamdy has made a few subtle changes to the original ingredients to give them extra flavours of excellence."

She so wanted to please the barman. She wanted him to stay with her, laugh with her and be part of her. She did not notice her dry throat as she took a bite of the pitta bread and allowed the falafel to roll down her tongue, without being chewed, and into the back of her throat. Had her throat not been so dry the falafel would have slipped comfortably into her stomach. Instead it lodged itself in her larynx, like a cork at a bottle's neck.

Instantly she choked. The remains of the pitta contents spluttered from her mouth. She shot to her feet, knocking her chair and table in different directions and, with her hands, she gripped her throat as the pain of not being able to breath tortured her wild eyes. In an instant motion she rocked backwards and forwards, consciously knowing that she had to breath air quickly. Her body was being starved. Her throat had to be freed and her lungs allowed to fill.

Sam had been shocked by the sudden incident. He had not really witnessed anything so dramatic and horrifying before, only the nanosecond flash of Billy's image under the truck mirrored through his mind before his instinct took over. He grabbed the girl, one hand wrapped round her stomach whilst the other thudded her back.

"Come on, let it out," he shouted. "Hamdy, get the jeep," he yelled. Again he hit her, this time harder but she continued to wrench herself jerking and tugging in desperation.

The situation was hopeless. He could see that no attempt on his part was going to release whatever the girl had swallowed. In his mind there was no alternative. He just had to get her to the hospital. Time was not on his side and he had to make that extra effort. With both arms he grabbed her failing body, his legs pedalling his shoes along the ground in their effort to reach the jeep. Hamdy had been quick. The jeep's motor was roaring alive in wait and, as Sam lurched in with the girl, he shoved his accelerator foot to the floor and sent the engine screeching forward.

Fortune was on Sam's side as they sped along the road. Eilat was a very small town with very little traffic, only a few roads with scattered houses and very little of anything else. There was no time for obstacles and road hold ups. The girl had to be attended to with frightening urgency; time was slipping away. Sam looked down at her and even through her twisted face he could see her beauty, the tears rolling down his face as he vainly prayed for the distant miracle.

"Faster Hamdy," he screamed. "Faster, she's losing it. Her face's blue. She's staring. Quick Hamdy, quick." He shouted on and on until finally the jeep crashed to a stop and almost drove through the hospital doors. Sam leapt out with his dying bulk, running and running down the corridor looking for help.

A nurse was pushing an empty trolley as Sam slammed into it. "She's stopped breathing, food trapped in her throat, she needs help," Sam so wanted to impress on the nurse the horrifying urgency.

"What's her name?" she asked.

"She's the girl who's going to be my wife." Sam's heart called out.

***

Shoshana had finished her rounds. The day had been relatively quiet with very few patients needing attention and for the first time in a long while she felt on top of her work and up to date with her reports.

Ever since she moved to the hospital she had built up the small surgical unit into an efficient working area where small operations and procedures could be carried out in absolute safety. The locals had applauded her good work with many letters of thanks and gratitude, from a baby's family for giving it life, a boy's parents for saving his and from children and grandchildren for coming to their parents' aid. The list was long as was very apparent from the many letters and pictures displayed with honour on her office wall.

She was content. She had her life again and, for the first time in the last few years, she was able to breath a sigh of relief and joy. She had met a handsome man. She was in love and, as a dividend, her daughter had come home. Yehooda would have been pleased for her and would have wished her a good life. His memory was always in her heart and his thoughts guided her forward.

Rounding the corner she met the oncoming trolley head on and was almost flattened by its impact.

"Doctor, doctor, she's stopped breathing. Her husband rushed her in. There's food trapped in her throat." The words stumbled out of the nurse.

Instantly, Shoshana recovered from the knock, her trained eyes scanned the damage whilst her mind geared itself for action. The patient was asphyxiated, had blue fingertips, blue lips, a pale face and there was no sign of breathing.

"The emergency bag, fast," she commanded the nurse. It had been the hospital management's policy to keep emergency bags filled with instruments at regular places and throughout the hospital for such crises and this urgency was no exception.

Shoshana knew by experience that time was fading. It was too late to attempt to remove the trapped food through the mouth. She would have to perform a tracheotomy, cut directly into the trachea and let the air in. From the emergency bag she removed a scalpel and braced herself for the cut. Only then, and to her horror, did she register the person lying on the trolley. Shoshana's eyes glared, her eyeballs almost popping out, her brow tortured with pain. There below her lay her dying daughter.

***

Flashes of lightning thoughts darted across Shoshana's mind, almost like ping-pong balls bouncing haphazardly inside a bingo caller's drum. Then she saw images of Yehooda's body on her surgical table, lying limp and lifeless. She remembered her panic and her guilt and thought about all the pointless medical training that left her confused. Question after question bounced haphazardly in an ever-increasing momentum, her mind stained with memories as she fought for relief. She had not been able to help Yehooda. Was this the repeat of the past? How was she going to help Sheba? The questions flooded in.

With a reflex action she made an incision into the trachea just below the larynx, cleared the hole with her gloved finger and inserted a tracheotomy tube. Instantly, air rushed into the empty lungs, filling them with its miracle contents before being forwarded to the heart. Within seconds Sheba's body reacted positively to the fresh air and recovered from death's doorway. It went from blue to pink and from trauma to calmness. Shoshana transferred her attentions to Sheba's mouth and with the aid of a laryngoscope opened the back of the throat, inserted a pair of forceps and removed the blockage. Her final act was to take out the tracheotomy tube, administer a stitch and place a plaster over the wound. Only then did she pause to correlate the whole nightmare, the jigsaw of terror and its noodles of entanglement. Fate had not struck a second blow; she had saved her daughter's life and was not damned.

Their eyes met.

"Sheba are you OK?" Shoshana exploded in delight at seeing her daughter's eyes and face more relaxed.

"Mum, what happened? The last time I remember anything, I was eating falafel and the next moment I was choking," Sheba stammered in trying to remember.

"Oh, darling, you're fine; you'll be all right. This little devil," Shoshana mused as she held the falafel up for Sheba to see, "lodged itself in your throat. Thank goodness someone...." She paused mid-sentence 'her husband rushed her in', the nurse had said. The words tumbled out of Shoshana's inner conscience mind as if they had been held in place for future analysis. "Your husband?"

"Yes, he's waiting outside," the nurse informed them.

***

Sam sat drumming his fingers, his feet shifting uncomfortably whilst his head bowed down in wait of news of the girl's condition. At the same instance he was cursing himself for not having the ability to help her. He was so frightened and so distressed by what he had witnessed and traumatised at the thought and consequences of such an accident. He would never forgive himself and would always take the blame should she not pull through the ordeal.

From the first moment he had seen the girl in his bar thoughts of pleasure had flooded his senses. Never had he witnessed such strength of feelings, such might and force. Yet all the while he knew and hoped from the sparkle of her eyes that she had mirrored his power and shared his feelings.

He began to pace the room. The waiting was exhausting; he just could not bear another minute of hanging around. He had to find out, he had to know immediately how she was. Bursting through the doors he marched down the hallway and thundered into the side room.

The nurse was the first to recover from the shock of his outburst. "Your wife is fine," she exclaimed.

"Sam!" stammered Shoshana on her recovery.

"You know him?" queried Sheba in amazement and in a louder voice.

"Are you married?" replied Shoshana in an even louder voice.

***

She placed her arms round his waist, her firm legs round his thighs as they pulled together, holding tightly and swaying rhythmically. The pleasure was so intense, their minds locked in ecstatic mode with pictures of euphoric thoughts, enormous enjoyment and satisfaction. He buried his face into her soft bosom, sucked and licked her firm nipples. She lowered her hands, her fingers gently running down his sides and her nails lightly scratching the pores of his skin. Her hands pressed more firmly as together they reached the climax and pinnacle of their desires.

Freefall ended. They floated back to Earth, exhausted and relieved of their needs. They were fulfilled and bliss had wrapped their shattered bodies, all energy sapped from their souls. They fell asleep.

Jack had always felt a deep desire for Shoshana from the moment he had sighted her at the kibbutz. Her beauty had etched an image of want and yearning into his mind, a craving for touch which he could not bear nor wanted to ignore. He could tell, and hoped, from the way she had gradually accepted his friendship and leant on him for advice and comfort, that she had similar feelings for him.

Shoshana had not looked for, nor wanted another relationship. The scars of Yehooda's death were too deep and hurtful. She preferred to hide from any new entanglements and chose to keep herself at arms length. However, she had not accounted for the power of Jack's attraction. Just being with him was a temptation too difficult to ignore. With passing time their relationship bloomed, as did Shoshana's acceptance of Yehooda's death. In relaxing her guard the two became close friends and the day the two became lovers was the first day of Shoshana's new life.

They lay, as stacked spoons on their sides, in harmony and completely at peace with their lives, both shattered from their lovemaking and slackened from their uncoiled sexual hunger. They fell asleep

Jack woke with a start, his senses alive and his inner clock ringing the time. He was alert to the task he had set himself.

***

Sharing duties was a necessity in kibbutz life and Jack was certainly not one to shy from his responsibilities nor refuse to take on extra chores. In fact the knowledge of his enthusiasm was so well etched into the minds of every Eilot kibbutznik member. They all respected his vitality when it came to volunteering. His duty of looking after the fire-fighting and safety equipment bore the hallmarks of his eagerness and determination to seek improvements at every opportunity.

Jack's moment of fame was realised at the monthly management meeting when he fought for the replacement of the antiquated water-tower. The existing tower with its deep cracked wooden supports, once rigid and firm, was weakened by the combination of wind, blasts of sand grains, burning sun and icy nights. It looked as the Tower of Pisa might do before toppling.

Jack had repeatedly warned of the possible danger and collapse of the water tower and of the latent harm to children playing in its shadow. The school stood yards from the tower as did the community hall. Both lay in line and, should disaster strike they would suffer the brunt of any flood.

The tower defied Jack and, in spite of a number of minor earthquakes and nature's rumbles, it survived. As if almost toying with Jack's feelings it stayed upright to tease and mock. It became an obsession and Jack would not be defeated.

His mind was made up. There would be no turning back, no recriminations and no second thoughts. He would solve the problem and suffer the consequences. As far as he was concerned the children's safety was paramount. The tower had to make way for a more modern and safer construction.

Having woken up, he was ready.

In the midst of night, well after sunset, the moon at its smallest smile and the shadows at their thickest shades, Jack went armed with his saw. The uprights gave little resistance to the teeth, as one by one they were half sawn. With a rope fastened to the highest beam Jack pulled the tower to the ground. It gave little resistance.

***

Jack settled under the comfort of the sheets and back into Shoshana's arms. His face portrayed the smile of satisfaction as his mind replayed the sight of the falling water tower and the spillage of its contents over the roadway and into the adjoining vine field. The ripening grapes must have been surprised and pleased from their extra fill.

As he continued to grin, his thoughts toyed with the incoming morning, the reaction of the kibbutz and the confusion that would prevail. And yet, he was not worried. "What could they do, even if they suspected him, how could they prove it was him? Anyway, it was inevitable. The tower would have eventually collapsed and he had just brought the date forward a little.' he continued to muse to himself.

News of the collapsed tower flooded through the kibbutz with a force similar to that of the spilled water. Some members deplored the catastrophe whilst others quietly applauded the knowledge that, at long last, the danger had been averted.

"Did you hear about the water tower?" Shoshana enquired the following day as the two sat for dinner.

"I believe it collapsed during the night," Jack smiled his reply.

"You don't say," she chuckled. "So tell me, couldn't you sleep? You were tossing around all night. You just wouldn't keep still and from the depth of my sleep I somehow remember you getting up," continued Shoshana. "And do you know what? I remember hearing the front door lock click, the handle scrape and the hinges creak open. Bring any memories your way?" She persisted, almost toying with him. She had suspected Jack's intentions but somehow had never thought that he would actually go the whole way and pull the tower down. She giggled, her eyes shut and projecting several images against her eyelids of Jack rustling his way in the shadows, sawing the supports and lassoing the tower down.

"You did it didn't you?"

"I did not"

"Yes you did, admit it," Shoshana laughed, wagging her finger at him and reaching over to pinch his nose.

"What awful things could you be thinking about," he winked and burst into laughter.

The two giggled and laughed and as Jack reached over and held Shoshana's hand he was overcome by her vision. She was so beautiful, her eyes were wide with fun and joy. Her soft pink cheeks and gently sloping nose, her full lips parted with excitement as her fine hair floated across her face. She was perfect, a picture to cherish and hold sacred forever. He stood up and pulled her to him. Softly they kissed, lips slightly parted to feel their electric tongues connected as one. They were in love.

"Will you marry me?"

Chapter 8

"Marry me."

Sam had taken ages to build up his courage. He barely knew her name, where she came from, who she was, what she did, what she liked or what made her laugh. There were so many unknowns, so many queries and yet he knew from the moment he had seen her at the bar she was the one he wanted to spend the rest of his life with.

"I don't know you. This is very embarrassing," she shied, her eyes glued to his. How could she make such a decision? Could she leap into the dark, blindfolded and reckless? Then what if they were wrong for each other, incompatible, had different ideas and feelings, different likes and dislikes? What if he did not care, did not want commitment, did not look after her nor show desire, excitement and thrill? The questions just rolled and rolled in her mind, searching for answers as they bombarded one another.

"I'm Sam Silo," he smiled at her beautiful face. His finger brushed a strand of hair lying loosely over her cheek. He felt her smooth skin, so soft to the touch, so tender and appealing. "I'm still struggling with your language. You'll have to forgive me," he mused. "So where should I begin to tell you about my life, the life I left behind and the new-born me, in a world at the other side of the globe where everything you see or do is completely different from the way life is here." Sam recalled life in Liverpool, the love he shared with his mother and the hatred he felt from his father, the pals from school days, the good times and those days he remembered wishing himself dead. Then his thoughts went to the moments leading up to being scooped up with the cotton bale and plunged into the hellhole of the ship's hold.

"Billy came to my rescue. Oh, he was such a friend, the best you could wish for, like a big brother who looked after me." Sam's eyes watered as he continued to recall the perilous journey, their close encounter with death's door, the bandits, the mad watermelon truck driver and the desert terrain. He recalled their arrival at the shores of the Red Sea in Eilat, their struggle at the mines and the tragedy of Billy.

Sam paused for a while.

"How awful! What a dreadful journey you had," Sheba reached over and held Sam's hands. She gently cradled his fingers, interlocked her knuckles with his and softly squeezed to show her deep feelings of care and affection.

Sam looked up. His eyes sparkled into Sheba's gaze and he wanted to tell her so much more about his hopes and his wishes.

"Billy was my strength, my stronghold. Everything I did in Eilat was with him and for him. When he died I almost died with him. Then, like a blessing, your mother brought me back to life. She showered me with new strength and, through her dramatic experience with your father, helped me to be positive and see the future ahead."

Then Sam told her of the future and of the determination he had sworn himself to achieve for Billy's namesake.

"I want Billy's bar to be famous. I want the world to know that Billy was the one who saved my life, the one who has spurred me on to do great things and the one without whom I would not have met this wonderful, beautiful and sweet smelling rose of perfection." Sam pulled Sheba closer to him, their lips almost touching and their pupils wide and deeply staring. "Will you marry me?"

There was only a wish, a premonition, a sixth-sense feeling that this was right and he was her dream and reality. She did not want to lose him. She could not let him go. He had come all this way and destiny had dawned. They were made for each other, fated to be together and united in joy and loving happiness. This was right for them and together they would achieve greatness, bring up a family and live forever.

"I will," she yelled.

***

So commenced Sam's year of intensive learning and understanding of the Jewish religion. He wished to be accepted as an orthodox Jew and be allowed to marry with the blessing of a Rabbi and the kibbutz. Although he had reasonably mastered the language, reading was a greater barrier, requiring his extra effort and attention.

Sheba was a good teacher, taking Sam through the many festivals as and when they arrived on the annual calendar, firstly New Year around September, followed by Yom Kippur and the favourite festivals of Succoth, Simchat Torah, Chanukah, Purim and Passover.

He learnt of the mystique of all the festivals, the traditions that were the backbone of their customary beliefs. The Torah readings that accompanied the many periods of historical Jewish life engrossed Sam, as did the many breathless stories of disasters, achievements and of great success. He heard tales of the creation of the earth, the Garden of Eden, the Great Flood and Noah's Ark, the birth of Moses, the Ten

Commandments and the forty years of wandering.

Under the supervision of a Rabbi from Jerusalem Sam made the many journeys north required to complete the course of conversion and acceptance into the religion. He took to his study with enormous energy, regulating his life to the many religious obligations and ensuring he obeyed the laws as instructed to him by the Rabbi. The compass point of his direction always governed by the knowledge that ahead would be contentment, love and a future of religious acceptance for his family.

Often, during the months of intensive training when his energy was exhausted and his ambitious goals were at a low gear, he thought of giving up and nearly did but for the energy of Sheba who continued to stoke his waned reserves.

"I have good news," the Rabbi announced at an unexpected moment almost knocking Sam from his stool. "It's been a pleasure having you as a student. Have you set the date of the wedding?"

Chapter 9

'Hava Nagila' sounded across the hall, the band of four created the speedy tempo as the girl singer's voice drifted around its lively melody. The men were at one end of the hall and the women at the other, each spinning their circles of dance steps round and round, their feet pounding the floor. Arm in arm, arms over shoulders, hands hoisted upward, linked then unlinked, the group of dancers circled into many coiled springs.

Into the middle of the circles they jostled, then out and in again. As the music quickened so did the spinning dancers, into the centre and out like the ebbing and flowing of a stormy sea. Then as men linked arms they looped into figures of eight, left hand in and right hand in, left and right in time with the beat.

'Hava, nagila hava, nagila hava, nagila ve nismecha" the singer's voice boomed, over and over as a looping tape. Her voice strained to be heard by the dancing circles of elastic bands with each repetition. Two chairs were positioned at the midst of the frenzy, Sam and Jack, the grooms placed on them, lifted above heads and bounced. The two were holding hands and trying desperately to remain seated, as on and on the motion escalated. At the other end of the floor, Shoshana and Sheba were hoisted on their seats as their circle of female dancers echoed the men's gyrations.

"Ladies and gentlemen, your attention please, ladies and gentlemen," the echoing music would not allow the Chairman's words any space on the dance floor. "Ladies and gentlemen." Finally the music ceased, the two groups of dancers came to a stop and all eyes trained on the speaker.

"Today has been a most unique occasion in the history of the Kibbutz, the uniting of two sets of families, a double wedding of a mother, stepfather, daughter and son-in-law. Raise your glasses please and join me in wishing them a most happy and peaceful future.

***

"Sam, I'm going to introduce you to the real Israel. We're going on honeymoon," announced Sheba. Before he could muster words of being busy at work and not having time, she handed him their reservation bookings with a number of hotels taking them from the south to the north. "You may be able to drive from top to bottom in one day but it'll take you more than a year to see everything. We'll have to do it in a week and we're going in the morning."

No sooner had Sam completed his business arrangements, the two were in their car driving along the northern road, through the Negev Desert, along the Arava Valley to the Jordan Valley and the Dead Sea.

Sam's eyes glistened at the wonderful view of the area.

"So what do you think Sam? You're over 300 metres below sea level and standing by the saltiest sea in the world. Last one in," she raced off trailing her words, "is a loser."

Sam ran after her, caught her and was about to jump in.

"Stop. It's full of salt, idiot. Get that into your eyes and they'll sting you forever." Sheba guided Sam onto the edges of the sea and together they sat and leant backwards and then lay flat, floating along on a cushion of salt. Sam had not experienced such a feeling of lightness, nor of being able to float on water without the risk of submerging. He carefully pushed the surface of the water to move himself to a deeper area, his feet, stomach and head well above the surface. He held Sheba's hand and together they just relaxed in the sun's rays.

"Isn't this beautiful, so tranquil? It's like being in a huge bath, lovely warm water soaking all your troubles away." Sheba was so happy. "I love you."

"I love you more than you love me," Sam teased her.

"Come on, I've got something else to show you." In attempting to get up, Sam tried rolling to his side. "Not like that, stupid, you'll end up with a face of salt." She steered him closer to the edge. "Try now, it'll be much easier.

The thrust from the salt was so strong that getting out of the sea was no easy task. Sam placed his hand on the seabed. "Ouch, what the heck!"

"Those are large salt crystals. Be careful silly."

With a painful effort he forced himself upright. "Don't call me silly," he patted her bottom. "Where next? I'll race you." The two laughed as they ran ahead.

"The black mud," ordered Sheba, "over there where all those people are standing," she pointed as she ran faster with Sam chasing hard and close behind.

They joined the few other visitors who were busy spreading Dead Sea mud on their bodies.

"Here, let me cover you first and then you can do me," Sheba chuckled as she ladled handfuls of the mud onto Sam, covering all the skin areas. "It's good for blood circulation and keeps your skin soft and smooth, just like a baby" she giggled, rubbing his cheeks and pinching them. "A beauty face pack," she teased as she inspected her handiwork. "Now it's my turn."

Sam was pleased to oblige and in the style of Monet daubed mud all over her body using his fingers and arms as long brush strokes.

Once covered, they stood under the sun's rays and baked the mud to a crusty finish, as if in a kiln, and like stiff Mummies balanced themselves. They were only able to freely move their large round eyeballs, peeping white from their black faces.

Sam, looked around and to his amazement, there were clusters of families, groups of elderly people, groups of women, single men and many single women, all covered from head to toe in mud. If he had not seen it with his own eyes he would not have believed the popularity of the place. Everyone seemed to trust and worship the mud's benefits. He spoke to a few of the participants and was intrigued by their answers. Most said they came there several times a year to enrich and cleanse their bodies. Others, with ailments of arthritic nature, stiff joints and backaches, swore by the properties of the mud. To them it brought relief and eased their sufferings, like a miracle cure.

The shower soon washed the mud off and Sam also felt the comfort of a purified body and a clear mind.

They were ready to climb Masada.

"Come on, first one to the top."

"I don't know where you get all that energy from," called Sam as he chased after her.

"From running after those school kids of course."

Masada was no easy climb. The path wound upwards in a zigzag pattern, going steeper and steeper as it ascended.

"I took my oath of allegiance as a soldier on this mountain, 'Masada shall never fall again'," she recalled. "This is where the Jews rebelled all those years ago. They leapt over the edge to a certain death in defiance of being captured by the oncoming Romans."

"Aren't you a clever girl?" Sam caught Sheba by her shoulders pretending to push her off the cliff and then instantly pulling her back.

"Don't you dare." The two giggled, held hands and ran off.

***

"Where to next?" Sam was curious as to the next place on the itinerary.

"Tiberias, of course. It's further north."

On the way they rested from the sun under a grove of olive trees and on some soft grass. Sheba unpacked the picnic and they tucked into wine, cheese and salad.

"This is heaven," Sam whispered his pleasure as he lay on his back with Sheba leaning on him. "It's so beautiful and peaceful here."

They were lost in their piece of paradise, their minds drifting into a magically charged world of heavenly joy and total euphoria.

"Let's stay forever, just the two of us, side by side in the Garden of Eden."

"I wish," Sheba responded, "but we have to keep moving. We've still many miles to cover."

As Sam rose he felt a snip of a pain at the lower side of his back. "Ouch. What was that?" he exclaimed as he rubbed the sore area.

"Let's have a look," Sheba offered. "It's only a wasp sting; you must have been lying on it. Poor wasp!" she chuckled.

A red rash formed almost instantly and Sam's scratching intensified, as did the soreness. "It's quite bad and irritating. I need to put something on it to stop the itching."

"It's only a wasp sting, you'll live." Sheba could not help smiling at the thought of a little sting being so painful. Look, there's a farm in the distance, let's go and see if they can help.

Sam's itching had become so furious that he had caused the skin to rupture and bleed in parts.

"You must have had an allergic reaction to the sting but don't worry I've just the right sort of remedy for you," the lady of the farm offered. "Wait here, I'll just be a couple of moments." From her garden she cut a length of fleshy plant and brought it to Sam, she then slit a section across the bulkiest part of the stem and squeezed the sap gently out. It was like a thick oily liquid and as it dripped she spread it gently onto the sting and surrounding tender areas.

"Here, you have a go and while you're at it, spread it all over your body it will make your skin soft, and make it feel smooth and clean". Sam was amazed at the wonderful effect the sap had on his skin and how quickly the soreness subsided.

"What is that? It's like a wonder cream."

"Aloe Vera plant," offered Sheba, "here, let me rub some on my skin. It's been ages since I tried some and I remember last time my skin stayed smooth for ages."

The two said their goodbyes and once again thanked the lady for her help. Even after driving several miles, Sam was unable to clear his mind. He was astounded by the effect of the Aloe Vera plant and could not stop talking about it until they arrived at the banks of the Sea of Galilee.

"The Kinneret is named after a Kinor because the sea is in the shape of a violin," explained Sheba.

"Such knowledge from my brainy wife," Sam taunted.

Travelling north they saw many pilgrims making their way to the Galilee area in search of the Biblical history of the sea and surrounding land, following the footsteps of Jesus and visiting Nazareth, the home of Mary and Joseph.

Still further north, the two drove past Rosh Pinna, Safed the town of synagogues, and turned west to the resort of Nahariya, then back south through Haifa, Netanya, and Tel Aviv and finally back towards Eilat.

All the while Sam could not stop thinking about the mud and the Aloe Vera plant and its miracle sap.

Sheba could not help but notice Sam had been very quiet as she drove back to Kibbutz Eilot. In fact he had said about two words over a fifty-mile distance.

"Sam you're very quiet, are you dreaming?"

"No, I'm planning our future."

BOOK 2

Raymond Ross

Chapter 10

"Air France jet hijacked on routine flight to Paris." The bombshell news struck Israel and the world simultaneously. "Four terrorists boarded in Greece and hijacked Air France flight 139 during its journey from Ben-Gurion Airport to Paris," the news continued. "The pilot was forced to land in Entebbe where demands were made for the release of terrorists being held in Israel, France, Germany, Switzerland and Kenya in exchange for more than 100 Israeli and Jewish passengers."

Seven days later, the Israel Defence Force made a successful and spectacular rescue of the hostages in Uganda. History recorded the event as 'The Raid on Entebbe' in 1976.

***

The past few years had been very kind to Sheba and Sam, just as they had been to Shoshana and Jack. Both couples had settled in the kibbutz as neighbours and enjoyed their companionship.

The birth of a son for Sheba and Sam brought a third dimension to their love and pleasure.

"It's a boy and we've called him Billy." His name came without hesitation in memory of Sam's dear friend and lifesaver.

Life could not have been any better for the two families: Sheba continued with her teaching career, Shoshana became the hospital consultant, Jack managed kibbutz agriculture and Sam took Billy's Bar to new heights.

Sam unravelled the length of paper onto the bar and displayed his plans for the future. The dream and task he had set himself after losing his good friend was finally drawn as witness to his aspirations and determination to succeed. And, as he traced his fingers along the pencil lines his empire came to life. He would open Billy's Wine and Restaurant Bars throughout Israel, Jerusalem and Tel Aviv and as far north as Haifa.

Head office remained in Eilat where Billy's Bar was the largest, shaped as an octagon with doors leading to different cultures, one door to a Chinese banquet, another to an Indian, Mexican, Greek and the rest of Europe. And as diners walked through each of the doors they would be surrounded with the atmosphere and décor of the banquet style.

Hamdy and Magda continued to work with Sam. Their task was to control and tackle the many new demands placed on the business. As Sam expanded extra staff were employed, including cooks, waiters and bar hands to maintain the quality of service. Sam was no longer looking after the day-to-day management of the bars; the business had taken on a new dimension. His staff count had reached over one hundred serving thousands of meals a week and pulling twice as many pints.

Profits were up and gradually Sam was amassing the necessary funds to take him to the next stage of his dreams. The platform for growth had been set and he was ready for Billy's Bar to be in neon on hotels, stores and financial institutions. He would not rest until Billy was a household name.

***

Newspaper headlined the opening of the King Solomon hotel by an English entrepreneur. This was the first luxurious five star hotel, of the Isrotel Group, in the desolate town of Eilat and by the beach area.

The news caused an immediate response from travel organisations, with the tourist map of Eilat completely changing and transforming the resort into Israel's main leisure destination. It became a place for the whole of the world to focus on and realise the competition of an exotic sunshine experience.

With the demand air traffic quickly increased, El Al Airways serviced Eilat as the one destination everyone talked about and where travel critics proclaimed their delights of a heavenly location.

The sudden impact had investors streaming along for a piece of the action. The building industry came alive and installed other hotels, restaurants, water sports and entertainment. Tours were organised, such as a drive through the desert, a visit to a Bedouin settlement, swimming with dolphins, skiing and boating. The list was endless and the pace of renewal like an express train out of control.

****

"No more bets," announced the croupier as the hopping mad ball bounced from number to number and eventually landed in one groove to settle in peace. "Eighteen the winner," he announced as his arm shot forward to collect all the unlucky chips. The gentleman in the corner beamed another smile as his chip pile grew with every spin.

"Gaspov, the boss wants to see you. Yentev will take over the wheel."

Gaspov was pleased to have been called away from the table. After a three hour stint spinning the wheel and collecting chips his arms and legs felt fatigued and strained. However, the thought of having to go to see the boss was a little unnerving. He would rather have been resting at the bar and chatting up the new barmaid.

Gaspov made his way through the casino hall, across the bar and dining area to the stairwell leading to the deck below.

"Come in Gaspov. Sit down," commanded Rubchek.

Gaspov walked into the spacious room, his shoes sinking into the spongy woollen carpet leaving footprints as he proceeded to the large centrally positioned wooden desk. The little chair provided for him was designed to be towered over by Rubchek's as a way of belittling anyone who sat before him. The room was decorated in the utmost splendour of designer furniture, with velvety paper lining the walls, a glittering mosaic of ceiling lanterns illuminating every corner and multicoloured wooden panels adding light and dark shades to the perimeters.

Rubchek was merciless in his goal to succeed and certainly enjoyed to boast of the riches he had amassed. His bullying came easy as a consequence of his teenage years when, as a bare-fisted fighter, he left his competition bruised and broken. First in the ring and then as a drug baron in Central Russia, he coordinated an empire across the European borders. The movement of large quantities of cash and black money focused his attentions to casinos where cash could be laundered by the spin of a wheel and the turn of a card.

So began his armada of casino ships bordering many coastal resorts where crooks and gentlemen could mix, be entertained by luscious women, drink freely and be out of reach of the local authorities and the Law.

His gang of thugs would enter the ports and forcibly smash any establishment showing the slightest hint of competing. Casinos and whorehouses would be targeted and their clientele enticed with benefits of kindness to board his entertainment boats.

Rubchek had eyed the Red Sea as being a good location for entry into the Sinai Peninsula, Jordan, Saudi Arabia, Egypt and Israel, areas which he believed would become exotic locations for tourists.

Having established his casino boat in the Red Sea, he set out to exercise his power on the locals.

"Gaspov," Rubchek continued, "I understand you have a cousin living in Eilat and working for the authorities."

"A cousin? Er, you mean Mushka. I haven't seen her for years. I don't even know where she lives." Gaspov lied. He had always kept the existence of his cousin a secret from Rubchek, not trusting the bully and his thugs. Yet he could not help wondering how Rubchek had discovered her existence. He sat further back in his seat, gripping the arms even tighter with his white knuckles and dreading the next few minutes.

"Oh come on. Don't pretend you haven't seen her nor know of her whereabouts. You've been visiting her every Thursday on your day off. She lives at the far end of the town and works for the local authority."

Gaspov sat further back in his chair as blood stopped flowing into his whitened fingers and his knees began to shake.

"I have a little job for you," continued Rubchek, "I want you to contact her. I have something very important I want her to do and you're going to make sure she does it. Do I make myself clear?" Rubchek stood up as he delivered the final remark, towering even more over the cowering Gaspov. "Do I make myself clear?"

"I want your cousin to…"

***

"Happy birthday." The cheers sounded the coming of the candle lit cake. Billy took a long and deep breath as he held his head back and, with a sudden plunge, blew an almighty stream of air that sent the six flames out of existence. Again the familiar lyrics of 'Happy Birthday to you' echoed round the room and vibrated through the outer walls. The party had been going on for ages with almost every kibbutznik joining the celebration.

Billy had opened the many presents he had received, mainly schoolwork items, clothing and music tapes. The present that really caught his eye was from Sam and Sheba, a Star of David emblem, to wear on a gold chain around his neck. As he did so the star rested on his chest, shining and glittering from the sun. He loved it and swore never to take it off.

"OK who's playing football?" Sam only had to mention the word ball and instantly the party kids dashed out screaming in excitement. Some of the fathers came too and before long two teams were battling to score goals.

"This way, Billy." Shoshana called out, "kick it, look out, pass the ball." Even the grandparents had a go from the sides.

"How's your grandchild doing?" panted Sam as he took a rest at the sidelines.

"Ho what a player! I think he's going to be a professional when he grows up." Shoshana mused. "The rest of the kids can't keep up with him," and, just as she looked up at the field, "goal" the onlookers shouted. The kids ran over to hug Billy, the scorer.

"That'll make the other side play harder," announced Sam. "I'm going indoors but you'd better cheer harder. They're going to need a lot of luck to keep ahead." Sam disappeared off to the house.

Sheba was busy tidying up the party mess. Sam reached from behind, tickling her at the sides. Swivelling round, she gave him an almighty push against the settee and the two fell against the two soft cushions stacked against the back.

"I love you," Sam uttered the words, as he did every time they were together.

"I love you back," Sheba would reply. Then came the kiss and the long loving hug.

Whilst everyone was entertained outside the two sat together talking and laughing at the wonderful day their six-year-old son had given them, a day to remember and a day to hold onto for a long time. The luxury of being together was becoming more difficult as Sam's busy days grew greater. Billy's Bar demanded a lot more of his time which he spent travelling the length of Israel and attending many meetings.

"So Sheba. How would you like to be the owner of a hotel?"

" What do you mean?" she enquired.

Sam gave a smirk of a smile.

"A prime piece of land is being offered by the local authority, right next to the King Solomon Hotel and by the beach. Oh, it's just a wonderful position and whoever gets it will make a fortune," continued Sam. "Can you imagine it? We could make it the most prestigious hotel, fit for kings and, in the middle we could have Billy's Bar done up in grand style. Never mind about Paris, New York or London. This is where the wealthy would come," Sam continued to dream.

"Anyway, at the moment it's still to be decided. The authorities have asked for interested parties to put in a tender bid for the site and I suppose the highest price will be the winner. There's a lot of interest and it's going to be quite a contest, even the Isrotel group has indicated an intention to enter the race."

The following day Sam put in his bid.

Chapter 11

Mushka sat typing the many letters dictated to her by her principal, Ward Phillips, of Phillips and Sons, whose premises undertook the administration and control of all land and building regulations for the area of Eilat. Her swivel chair rocked in pace with her tapping fingers and her oak desk vibrated as if shivering with fright from excessive wear and tear. Her office, a bare box room, was just big enough to house the spilling files of property and land deeds on offer.

The office was experiencing its busiest time with new developers arriving in Eilat during the day. Some developers were prospecting and researching the areas potential whilst others were more purposeful and direct in taking risks and buying into the area. Those who took the risk stood to gain the most while the hub and exhilaration of the pace of change was only just at its infancy.

The office was busy with the offer of a new plot of land, next to the King Solomon, which was being made available for hotel developers. Mushka correlated all the information and sent out tender forms to all submissions. She was responsible for receipt of the bids and for forwarding the same to her boss for final contracts.

The door opened. She looked up.

"Gaspov, how lovely to see you." Mushka rushed up to give her cousin a hug. "I wasn't expecting you till Thursday. Here sit down I've just a few more letters to type." Then she noticed Gaspov's sullen face, like ash from dying embers. "What's the matter, are you all right?"

"Mushka, we have a problem. Oh this is terrible, a nightmare and I don't know how we're going to get out of it. Mushka, dear Mushka." Gaspov went over to hold her hand.

"It can't be all that bad."

"It is. Remember me telling you about the boss I work for, Rubchek? His bullying gangsters have been following me on Thursdays. He knows all about you. He knows you're my cousin, where you live and where you work. Oh Mushka, dear Mushka," tears welled in Gaspov's eyes as he related the meeting he had with the boss and the demands he made on him. "I feel so weak and helpless."

"Here, sit down. Wait, I'll just get you a drink." Mushka poured a drop of vodka into a small glass and encouraged Gaspov to sit. "Now, very slowly tell me what's the matter."

"It's all to do with that plot of land next to the King Solomon Hotel, the one being offered for development. Rubchek is determined to get the site; he wants you to make sure that his bid is accepted. He wants you to tell him the value of the other bids so that his will be the highest." The vodka calmed his nerves as he continued, "I told him it was impossible and that your boss would find out and he wouldn't get away with it. He's a monster, Mushka. His gangs go around terrorising people if they don't do what they're told. This is terrible. I don't know what to do."

"Well he's not going to frighten me, bully or no bully. I'm not going to let him trample over this office and he's certainly not going to ruin my career. Anyway the bids come into the office sealed. They are opened in front of witnesses. There is no way I could know the amounts in advance. Look you go back to tell him that it's impossible. Tell him that I would like to help him but I don't have access to the information. It would be impossible for me to tell him the figures."

For ages the two talked over the problem and concluded that Gaspov was to go back to Rubchek and explain, in the nicest way that Mushka would like to help him but she had no access to the bids and that a committee of officials controlled them. He was also to say that if she overheard any mention of values then she could pass that information on.

Gaspov went back to the casino.

***

The days seemed to get longer for Mushka. Her office work was so demanding. The news her cousin brought made her more tense than usual. She just could not believe someone could demand that she compromise her position in the office. Try as hard as they might and use whatever method of bullying they chose, she would not submit to the threat.

That night she was relived to settle into a hot soothing and bubbly bath to relax, close her eyes and let the temperature of the water evaporate her tensions.

She did not hear the front door being prised open, nor the footsteps that followed but felt the draught of air as the bathroom door swung fully. The huge thug growled like a rottweiler as he charged in. She tried to scream but his enormous webbed hand muffled the sound whilst the other dragged her naked body out of the bath and flung her on to the marbled floor. In her attempt to get up, first on one knee then the other he grabbed her from behind, flung her over his shoulders and carried her into the sitting room. There he flung her onto the central rug and as she landed on her back the air exploded from her lungs like a pressure cooker blowing its top.

He dropped above her and with an instant whipping swipe caught his palm across her face, stunning her momentarily. She franticly kicked her ankles between his sprawled legs, catching her thigh on his crotch and causing a moment of pain to flash through his sensitive areas. He winced before blasting another swipe on her cheeks. She collapsed exhausted: He removed his trousers, forced her legs apart and proceeded to rape her. Once satisfied, his desires met, he stood over her pale and limp body.

"Rubchek never takes no for an answer. He sent this message to you in case you were thinking of letting him down." Then he pulled a revolver from behind his waist, pointed at her foot and pulled the trigger.

***

All night she lay on the floor, without energy and totally spent, going in and out of consciousness. Her body was unable to muster a single ounce of strength to roll over or to crawl for help and, as the sun began to rise outside, neighbours walking past on their way to work could not have known her desperate plight.

Finally her senses returned and she was able to drag herself to the telephone to dial for help.

She could not get out of the hospital fast enough. When she recalled the threat on her life, her whole body shook. Goose pimples shivering to life every time she thought of the animal at her flat, the rape and the bullet. She was lucky. It was a warning. Her life nearly extinguished, she had no choice. Rubchek was going to win the day.

She hobbled with two sticks under her armpits as supports to the plaster the doctors had secured on her injury. The plaster would need six weeks to be of any use, but she did not even have two weeks. Bids were already being made for the site and she had little time to look after the Russian.

Arriving at her office, she quickly checked the post before reaching for the envelopes with the bid contents. There were two on her desk, with a further four expected, and with only five days left for the closing date.

Slowly she mulled over the outer envelopes, flipping them over and over and wondering how she would prize them open without detection. They were sealed with candle wax and stamped with her office's embossed badge across the face.

The pieces of a plan began to jigsaw together in her mind as she pictured herself using a sharp knife to ease the opening of the glued flap at the other end of the envelope and away from the waxed seal.

The two envelopes came apart easily and she made note of the bids contained before carefully re-sealing. Her fingers shook nervously in rhythm to a gigantic orchestra whose drums and symbols vibrated their harsh and escalating sounds. She had never been so nervous and frightened before nor had she ever had her life so violently threatened. Every time she heard a creak or shuffle of feet she thought of the worst and expected the thug to be back for more.

The first envelope was from Billy's Bar Organisation, a local address she noticed on the headed paper. The second was from a Spanish family, represented by Carlos Gómez who gave a central Eilat hotel address for reply.

She passed the information to Rubchek.

***

"So how do you rate our chances of acquiring the land adjacent to The King Solomon Hotel?" enquired Hamdy, who was very keen on the idea of running a restaurant and bar within a hotel complex. He could just see himself and Magda, organising the staff, making sure the tables were in place for the many diners and hotel visitors, sorting out the décor, the background music, the menu and the drinks. The list was endless in his mind but Magda would help him and together they would make it the greatest eating experience in Eilat. He could just see the crowds queuing for more.

"I'm not sure," replied Sam. "Somehow I just can't get a feeling of the right value to bid. There are no guidelines and this is new territory. When I sent the bid I toyed with lots of figures but at the end could only come up with a figure we can afford and be at ease with. It may be low for some but pitched just at the right value for us. We're just going to have to wait patiently for the results."

Sam could not accustom himself to having to make blind bids for something he so dearly wanted. He was more used to going direct, straight to the core of his determination to succeed. He always calculated his moves and was able to face all situations squarely and broadly in his pursuit of prosperity. However, this position left him restless and without a firm ground. He felt a little exposed, as if he were wondering in a desert with a compass whose pointer was missing.

He would also have to be patient and await the result of the bids.

***

Another two bids landed on her desk and again she carefully looked at their contents. There was a bid from an English property company, Davies Properties represented by Robert Davies who was also staying in Eilat and waiting for the announcements. From what she could tell Davies Properties had interests in a number of European countries and were hoping to expand into the Middle East. The fourth bid was from Moshe Gold of Tel Aviv, a lawyer acting on behalf of his family.

She passed the information to Rubchek.

***

Billy was a good boy, very attentive in the classroom and ahead for his age when compared with his contemporaries. Not only was he bright in the classroom but also excelled in most areas of sports. His good height gave him added power on the basketball court and as for front crawl, in the pool, he could not be outstripped.

Schooling in the Kibbutz was a communal experience, with the kids learning together and living in dormitories away from their parents. Billy hated being away from his mum and always took the opportunity of sneaking away at lights out, to quietly go to his parents' lodgings, crawl under the sheets and tuck himself between Sam and Sheba. In the morning they would shoo him back to his own quarters before he was discovered absent.

Billy spent much of his time with a couple of his friends who were a little more adventurous and who liked a mischief or two to spice up their day. On adults' nights, when the children were meant to be asleep, sometimes the main projector was brought out to the open field adjacent to the communal building and converted into a temporary cinema. Billy and his friends would climb the few trees surrounding the field for a bird's-eye view of the film.

They were very rarely detected and in fact some of the adults ignored the children thinking that they posed no trouble. The parents knew they were there even though the kids believed they did not. To them it was an adventure being in the trees, let alone having the bonus of seeing a film.

When Billy was not with his friends, he would take his bicycle along the narrow paths meandering the kibbutz grounds. The path took him along the fruit plantation, through the vineyards, the orange groves and apple orchards. Billy would cycle round the trees and bushes, as if on an adventure route circling the kibbutz like he was on a motor racing track full of 's' bends and sharp corners. Then there would be the straight parts where he could really let off steam and unwind his coiled springs, his legs peddling in ever increasing speed. He had often timed himself and on good days could complete a lap in 20 minutes. On bad and murky days time could just escape into hours.

Billy always cycled alone.

***

The last bid landed on her desk and for a moment she stared at it before picking it up and holding it in the air as if weighing the contents. Mushka slowly and delicately forced open the lower-end flap, just as she had done with the previous tenders. She took out the form, made a note of the bid offer, against which she wrote the name of Arthur McGregor. She then proceeded to glue the bottom envelope flap back down in its original position. Only a careful eye would spot that the envelope could possibly have been interfered with.

She passed the information to Rubchek.

Chapter 12

Rubchek sat upright in his heavy armchair. He looked at the bids listed on the sheets sent to him by Mushka and at the names alongside. From the five bids, two were ridiculously high whilst the other three had reasonable tones. It was important that when he submitted his envelope the price would be the best and the one chosen.

He had no problems with the three lower bids; he could easily pitch his price at a slightly higher amount without any problems and still keep within his budget.

It was the two ridiculously higher bids, which caused him much aggravation, irritation and annoyance. He would have to sort out Carlos Gómez from Spain and Arthur McGregor from Scotland.

He made the first of the two telephone calls.

***

"Is there anything else I can get for you Mr McGregor?" the smartly uniformed waitress enquired as she placed his first course on the laced tablecloth in front of him. She had already shaken his cotton-starched serviette across his knee and placed the correct cutlery for the first two courses ordered. For lunch he had requested chicken soup with lots of noodles and a medium to well-cooked steak with a side-salad, two vegetables and a portion of chips. She also placed a bread roll and pat of butter on his side plate.

"No thank you," he replied

McGregor was familiar with Israel. He had travelled the whole area from north to south as a consultant in his quest to satisfy his clients by locating investment opportunities in the Promised Land.

Recently he had negotiated a substantial property on Mount Carmel, overlooking the port of Haifa, for an American conglomerate. The deal was so successful that he was still riding high on his commission.

On hearing of the sudden tourism boost of Eilat, he raced over to scour the region for possible deals. By chance he walked into the offices of Gold and Goldman, estate agents and valuers who were involved in a number of acquisitions and building projects mainly in the mountain area where land was being flattened for the production of apartments. He met one of the partners, Marvin Goldman, who very kindly took him round some of the developments. Whilst they were enjoying a cool soda under an umbrella outside one of the town's bars, Goldman revealed to him that an area of shore land was being earmarked for hotel development. McGregor's ears pricked up at the mention of hotels, as this was the type of investment one of his clients requested.

On their return to the office, Marvin made a couple of telephone calls and was pleased to report on the offer of land adjacent to the King Solomon Hotel. Together they submitted their offer.

McGregor was feeling very elevated from the prospect of the construction work and reflected on the opportunity it would generate as he sat in the hotel's dining room munching his steak. The bid he and Marvin had formulated was a very substantial one and he knew that very few could match such an offer.

McGregor was right. Their bid was the highest.

***

In front of Rubchek's desk stood two of his trusted aides, nicknamed Scar 1 and Scar 2 for the terror they inflicted and for always leaving their signature marks by a crossed scar on the victims left cheek. In Russia there had been a number of bodies discovered bearing the scars and although the authorities knew of the nicknames they were never able to prove their findings.

The two were anxiously waiting to do his bidding and to exert whatever pressure he demanded of them to accomplish their tasks. They knew, from his expression, that great forces were brewing inside his mind and were about to detonate and explode.

"I have a little job for you," Rubchek informed them.

He handed them the address of Gold and Goldman.

***

They entered the tiny office bearing the partnership name of Gold and Goldman.

"Can I help you?" the secretary's voice was hardly on the decibel scale. She was taken back with a slight fear at seeing the two ogres trampling in. "I'm Nancy. Can I help you?" again she attempted to be heard.

"Your boss, Goldman, which is his office?" She didn't have to answer, her

131

eyes told everything as she glanced at the door leading to the centre office.

They marched in, knocking the door from its hinges and leaving its handle embossed into the adjacent wall. Goldman was as much surprised as his secretary had been when they first entered. He looked up just in time to see a fist raining at him, knocking his nose inwards and splintering his bridge bone apart. Blood squirted from his ruptured skin and whilst he tried to keep his feet from buckling the second punch landed across the side of his head. This time his skull caved in. He never rose again from such a blow. Scar 1 bent over and with his knife, marked a cross on Goldman's left cheek.

"McGregor's address," they snarled at the secretary. She panicked showing them the address book, and, as they left, she carried a single bullet in her forehead and a cross on her left cheek.

***

McGregor had finished his lunch and had wandered onto the terrace area for a quiet afternoon of reading. He was in no hurry; with no other projects in hand, he had put aside four weeks for holidaying whilst waiting for news of the bids.

The daily newspaper headlined a bus hijacking by eleven terrorists who came from Lebanon on rubber commando dinghies and landed at the beach of Kibbutz Ma'agan. They killed an American photographer and a taxi driver before hijacking a bus whose passengers included many children on a day trip to the north. On reaching a blockade along the Tel Aviv road, fighting broke out, the bus burst into flames, 35 people died and 100 were injured. Nine of the terrorists were killed whilst two were captured. The year was 1978.

Terrorist activities were a regular occurrence in Israel and McGregor was thankful that, in spite of the many trips he had made, he had not been at the receiving end.

Then he looked up. Two shadowy faces were looking down at him.

"Mr McGregor. Stand up and walk very slowly out of the hotel. We have a car outside. We need you to come for a little ride." Scar 2 prodded a handgun into McGregor's left side to encourage him to get up.

"What is this all about? What's going on? Have I done something?" the questions streamed along from McGregor.

"Be quiet, just walk." The gun prodded deeper into his ribs and as he winced from the pain his feet moved more quickly.

The car was driven to the premises of Phillips and Sons.

"Now this is very simple, McGregor. Together we are going into the offices of Phillips and Sons, you're going to ask them to return the bid envelope you left with them," instructed Scar 2. "Now don't forget I'm going to be right beside you with this automatic and, if you try anything foolish you can forget ever walking out alive. Do I make myself clear?" He prodded the gun further into his ribs. McGregor shot up in pain and almost doubled over.

"This is all very silly," winced McGregor. "It's only a bit of land, what harm is there in my bid and why should I want it back?"

"Move, or else! No more questions." Scar 2 had no time for silly talk. "I said move." With an almighty shove he pushed him forward up the path to the office.

Mushka looked up on seeing the men enter her doorway.

"Can I help you?" she enquired.

"Ah yes, I put a bid in for the piece of land by the costal area, the one for a proposed hotel development." The gentleman hesitated for a moment, only to receive an even sharper dig from Scar 2. "Well, I've changed my mind and would like to cancel the bid."

Mushka could not help but notice that the man before her had a troubled expression as if he were acting against his will. She also could not understand why the man behind was standing so close nor what the two had in common as they appeared complete opposites.

"Could I have your name please?" she requested, "so that I can locate the right envelope."

"It's McGregor."

Then it dawned on her. The gentleman before her was the one whose name and bid price she had given to Rubchek and the thug behind was probably one of Rubchek's hired gang. There was nothing she could do, as being too frightened from her recent experience she ceded to the request and handed back the offer envelope.

McGregor was led back to the car and as he bent his head to get in the barrel of the automatic smashed against his temple. He never recovered.

Chapter 13

Rubchek made the second call. It was to his Spanish contact.

"Ricardo, there is a little matter which I would like you to look after for me."

***

Ricardo travelled west from Malaga, along the main road parallel to the coastal area of Southern Spain. He enjoyed viewing the harsh changes of the landscape. To the right were high rugged mountains with peaks reaching above cloud level, whilst to the left were the roar of seacoast, the long miles of sand and stone beaches and the relentless ebbing and flowing of the tide and its battering waves.

The beauty of the area inspired his appetite for his intended task and, as he approached the little village of San Pedro, his adrenaline level rose to new heights. It was a small village with narrow lanes flanked by snakelike rows of houses, all attached and concertina squeezed. He knew the village well from his childhood days when his mother had visited her family.

He found the address easily and rapped on the door.

"Can I help you?" enquired Carlos Gómez's wife

"May I come in?" Ricardo entered the small hallway leading to the dining room before she could reply. "I have a message for you from your husband. Is there anyone else in the house?" he continued.

Being satisfied that she was on her own, he proceeded to take a pistol from under the inside of his jacket.

"Don't be alarmed. This is only a means of getting the job done. You will be safe if you follow my instructions."

She was rooted to the spot and had tried to catch her breath, in terror from seeing the end of the barrel pointed squarely at her head.

"Now just sit down, this will only take a minute. I am going to telephone your husband and as long as we can persuade him to do a little job for us, then I'll be gone in a whisk."

Ricardo picked up the telephone and began to dial.

***

"Who can that be ringing the doorbell?" Carlos enquired of himself. He had just sat down for a rest, to put his feet up after a trying morning at the Bank Hapoalim. Not only were the queues so long but also when he did speak to a representative he had to be referred to two others before he could even begin to transfer currency from his Spanish bank to Eilat. The experience had been exhausting and at one time he thought he was going to have to change to dollars first, a currency the Israelis preferred.

Even the air-conditioning in the bank had been against him, a worn out fan blade dying on the system just when the day's temperature had pushed above 100 degrees. The banks main lounge was sweltering within seconds of the breakdown, which affected the service the staff could offer and ultimately resulted in the long wait.

He had no choice. The funds had to be available should he be successful in the bid offer for the piece of land with planning permission for a new hotel development.

The doorbell sounded again this time followed by a firm knock. He went to answer.

"Mr Gómez? Hallo, I'm Erickson. Your wife sent me with a message for you. She wants to talk to you on the phone. May I come in?"

He did not wait for a reply and walked straight to the telephone sitting on the side table by the doorway. He picked up the receiver and dialled.

"It's your wife. She wants a word."

Carlos was taken aback by the incident, not knowing how to react and not sure what was going on.

"Hallo, is that you, Carolina?" His wife burst into tears on hearing her husband and her name.

"Carlos, oh Carlos," she continued in tears. "There's a man with a gun sitting next to me. He says you must do everything he wants you to or he will shoot me. Carlos I'm so fright.." Her voice tapered off as the handset was snatched from her grip.

"Mr Gómez the gentleman who is with you will tell you what you must do in order to stop me from killing your wife." The line went dead.

"Sit down, Mr Gómez," Erickson commanded.

As he sat, his face had turned ashen. His eyes looked with terror and his mind was numbed by the thought of his wife being harmed.

"Tell me what you want me to do. Please, don't hurt my wife," he pleaded

"I am going to drive you over to the offices of Phillips and Sons. When we get there you are going to go to their reception and ask to be given back your bid envelope, informing them you've changed your mind and no longer require the site for development. Do you understand?"

"This is ridiculous. You're threatening my wife's life for a bit of land. It's absurd. Does it mean so much to you?"

"It does and you're going to help us by saving your wife's neck. So, let's get started."

They drove to Phillips and Sons and parked the car.

"Can I help you?" enquired Mushka on seeing Carlos enter.

"Yes I submitted a bid for some land for the purpose of building a hotel but I have changed my mind and would like to take back my bid envelope."

"Let me have your name and I'll see if I can find the envelope."

"It's Carlos Gómez."

Mushka immediately recognised the name as the one she had reported about. Once again she felt terrified just thinking of Rubchek and she chose to ignore her emotions and not to say anything to the gentleman before her. She felt safer keeping as far away from the situation as possible.

Carlos returned to the parked car and handed over the envelope.

"If you don't mind I'd rather walk from here."

Proceeding along the main street of Eilat, Carlos walked towards the airstrip at the bottom of the hill and towards the coastal area. He felt so much better knowing that Carolina would be released. He would never compromise her safety for a piece of land, no matter how much money was involved. So if he could not make this deal he would make another.

His motto was 'if it was meant to happen it would'. In this case it was not meant to happen.

He was so engrossed in his thoughts, he did not notice Erickson's car speeding towards him. It mounted the pavement and mowed him down.

***

The following day, in the local newspaper, two minor incidents were reported and on different pages. The first incident was of a Spanish businessman, by the name of Carlos Gómez, who was killed by a runaway vehicle. The second incident was of a Scotsman named McGregor, who was battered to death whilst being robbed.

When Mushka read the two names she almost fainted. Not only had the two been to her office but also it was her information that had lead to their deaths. She cursed ever knowing Rubchek, the murderer and monster.

Had Mushka been given a copy of the San Pedro local newspaper, she would have read of a robbery incident in the village where a victim by the name of Carolina Gómez was murdered.

Raymond Ross

Chapter 14

Gaspov had been trying to see his cousin, Mushka, on a number of Thursdays but on each attempt he had been given a duty at the casino. He began to believe that Rubchek was preventing him from seeing her.

Ever since he had gone back with the news that Mushka was unable to get the bid information there developed an air of uneasiness between himself and Rubchek. No longer was he given the good tables to croupier, but the less popular ones where tips were less generous and the hours of playing more inconvenient.

At least he was at peace, thinking that if the only consequences of Mushka not doing what was asked of her were for him to have a little discomfort at the casino, then they had got away with the problem very lightly.

Nevertheless, he did miss his Thursdays with her.

***

Rubchek was pleased with the outcome of his plans and the removal of the two highest bidders. The path was now clear. He completed his application bid offer under the cover name of 'Eilat New Build', a company he had formed some years ago for the purpose of seeming to be local and of having no Russian connection. It was also a company he could bring out of mothballs when the time was right. This was the right time. He was ready for his bid to be accepted by the planning department for the development of the greatest hotel complex in the world. He raised his arms in the air as if to welcome the sight. He could see in his imagination the modern structure towering over the horizon, standing above all others and being the master of buildings. As he believed he was the master over people.

***

Mushka was busy preparing the documents and paperwork for the meeting of bidders. At which time, the committee of judicators would announce the successful company to be awarded the offer of purchasing the lease, to the most sought after site for development.

Being very meticulous, Mushka wanted to ensure that every piece of document was in hand and accounted for. She made her way to the Authority's store rooms where records dating back to the year of independence were held.

The storeroom was only a short way from her office, but under the intense heat of a midday sun, the few minutes it took her to walk, seemed ages. The afternoon air was so dry. She felt as if she was being baked in a kiln from just walking across the road.

"Mr Fineburg, how are you?" she enquired of the storeroom keeper.

"All the better to see you," he smiled. "We don't have many visitors to this office and when a pretty girl walks in, well its like music to my ears."

"Well you know me. I got so tired sitting around in the office and thought,

I haven't seen Mr Fineburg for such a long time, why don't I visit him?" she grinned back

"You're welcome any time, my dear, and the more often the better."

"My god it's so hot in here," she suddenly realised. "I thought I was stepping out of the heat. I've never known the temperature outside to be so hot but I thought it would be a little better inside."

"Well it isn't. This building is older than me; it was never designed for modern use. It has musty smells and doesn't have air-conditioning. It's no wonder no one wants to visit. So, tell me what really brings you here?"

"There's a piece of land being offered for tender, right by the beach. They want to build hotel complexes for all the tourists expected in the area over the next few years." It was not a private tender so there was no reason for secrecy. "Anyway I'm trying to collect all the relevant documents for the area and I thought there may be some historical papers filed in your office: some maps, written agreements, documents. Well, I don't know, anything at all relating to the tender."

"Help yourself. But I warn you it's very hot in there and the lights are not much better. It's quite dark. Here take this torch you'll probably need it."

He had not exaggerated as, on opening the storeroom door, Mushka was greeted with a flow of very hot and stale air, as if it had been trapped for many years. There were rows and rows of worn out, dented green cabinets which were gathering dust at their feet. One beam of light shone through a tiny slot of a windowpane illuminating like a projector in a cinema. The light carried a swirl of dust particles in its circumference as if to mimic the eye of a hurricane, clear inside and monstrous on the outside.

She carefully stepped onto the dust-laden concrete floor and began to walk along the row of files. Luckily, they had been alphabetically marked, although in this case she was not sure as to which letter of the alphabet she needed. However, she thought she would start with 'L' for 'Land Rights'. With the help of the torch she flipped through a number of documents.

They were mainly relating to legal arguments put forward by eminent lawyers. She tried 'B' for Borders, 'D' for Disputes, 'C' for Coastal Areas, 'B' for Beach and on and on she continued as she gradually ran out of letters.

Having exhausted herself and, feeling well cooked with perspiration dripping on her, as from a sprinkling hose, she decided to come out of the depths of the room. She went past a row of cabinets standing almost at one side as if they had been singled out at class and sent to the corner for bad behaviour.

The cabinets had not been marked alphabetically but rather with more definite titles, one depicting 'Retail Building Specifications' and another 'Policies for Land Areas in Manufacturing'. The one that caught her eye was 'Barren Coastal Fields. She opened the drawer, after exerting some strain to her triceps and biceps. It was obvious that this drawer had not been opened for many years and the documents inside were very dog-eared and tanned from age.

She flipped through the files, and was interested to read information on the barren field developments around the coast, by Eilat and surrounding the Red Sea. However, in spite of learning some further insights into the historical make up of the area, nothing she had seen related to her present task.

She was about to close the drawer when her keen eye focused on a particular document. Her eyes widened with exhilaration. Her spirit danced with joy; she was elated with her discovery.

She hurried back to her office clutching an old document that was to change everything.

***

Arriving at her office, Mushka collected all her papers together. The meeting to award the lease on the site was due to take place the following day. There would be many representatives from the various authorities and agencies in attendance, anxiously waiting for the results to see if they could benefit from the many contracts which would be available.

Scanning through the bids, she confirmed her thoughts and quickly made a note of the address she needed to visit.

As she left her office she did not notice the white car following her.

***

Sam patiently waited at the hospital-parking bay, marked 'Ambulance Only'. He had received a request from Sheba, who was visiting her mother at the hospital, to pick up herself and Shoshana on his way home.

He had finished his day on a high, having met with Hamdy and Magda at the offices of Cohens Bakery. The company had promised to supply fresh bread and rolls on a regular basis but, over the previous weeks, their service had deteriorated. Part of the blame lay with the delivery agency. They were also asked to attend. Hamdy had become frustrated by the lack of co-operation from the company in sorting out their differences and asked Sam to assist in renegotiations.

The meeting lasted through the afternoon with each company blaming one another for the poor service. Finally, after many hours of negotiations and several warnings from Sam, the two companies settled their differences. The two capitulated and formulated a new timetable for the preparation and delivery periods.

The afternoon heat had been a hindrance to Sam who had never been able to acclimatise himself to such extreme temperatures. He was tired and sweaty, and as he sat waiting, he visualised a swimming pool. He saw himself diving into cool water, swimming a few lengths and splashing with his son, Billy. His son gave him wonderful pleasures of fatherhood and whenever he could he would take time off to be with him, encourage him in sports, education and discovery. He wanted to give Billy all the things he did not have as a growing son.

"Hi Sam, have you been here long?" He snapped out of his thoughts to see both Sheba and Shoshana at his car door ready to get in.

"I was just thinking of a cool swimming pool."

Putting the car into gear he slowly moved out of the hospital compound and onto the main road going north towards Kibbutz Eilot.

***

Mushka arrived at the address she had noted at the office. No one was at home, she felt a little deflated as she had an important message to impart.

The white car waited patiently, out of sight. The driver was straining with a pair of binoculars to keep a watch over her. Trailing her for the past few days had not been easy, especially in a hot tin motor.

She continued to wait

***

Sam rounded the corner past a white car parked on the side and up the drive leading to his house.

"There's someone sitting at our doorstep," announced Sheba.

As they neared their house, Mushka stood up in some relief from the wait.

"Are you involved with Billy's Bar?" she immediately enquired of Sam before he could string a sentence of "can I help you?"

"Yes." Sam could only think of one word in his surprise at her haste.

"I cannot stay long. I could be in great danger. Please take this envelope it carries some information which I think you will find helpful.

Before he could invite her into his home she was running to her car like a desperate vixen escaping from a hunt.

She turned the ignition and as her car came to life she headed back to town. The white car followed her every move.

***

Sam was left opening his front door in wonder of why the woman was in such a rush and why she looked so scared.

"What did she want?" enquired Sheba

"She was in such a hurry, poor thing looked so distressed," commented Shoshana. "What's in the envelope?"

"I don't know and, before you ask, I don't know who she is." Let's go in and then I'll open the envelope.

Raymond Ross

Chapter 15

The big decision date had arrived. The large public hall used for these occasions was made ready by the porters on duty, who with the direction of Mushka arranged a number of seat rows, strategically placed to keep the various opponents apart. On each seat she placed an agenda sheet and on some an extra card depicting the name of the person for whom the seat was reserved.

Due to the heavy interest in the area and growth of the travel industry, they were expecting many people in the audience. They knew that each of the bidders would be bringing an entourage of consultants, lawyers, accountants, planners, builders, architects, estate agents and anyone else who would give them advice on property and the hotel industry.

The back of the hall was reserved for the press. They expected representatives to be there from the whole of Israel, as if the world would be looking on, in marking the day as one big step in the world tourist map.

Mushka arranged a number of desks at the top area of the hall where the panel were to sit, together with glasses and a jug of water at each end. The meeting was scheduled to last approximately one hour but experience had taught her that some people were very inquisitive and liked to ask all sorts of questions. To them time was very elastic and, if pulled hard enough, could stretch for miles.

A note pad and pencil was added at the side of each of the panel seats, in case anyone wanted to take notes, together with ashtrays should the going be hard and they become stressed. A smoke was good for calming their nerves.

At 10.30 am people began entering the hall. Some were milling around to see if there was any indication as to whom the offer would be given, whilst others were content to stay the full course, not believing in hearsay but rather wanting to hear from the 'horse's mouth'.

By 11.00 am the room was full. Robert Davies, the building contractor based in Israel, sat on the front row towards the left, his lawyer seated at one side and a couple of bankers seated at the other.

Then Moshe Gold, the lawyer from Tel Aviv, sat on the right end of the row and next to his client and the client's accountant.

Rubchek made a dramatic entrance, accompanied by a couple of bodyguards, his lawyer, and accountant and property advisor. They looked a grumpy set of figures walking purposely to their seats in the middle section of the row. Not one of them smiled or even acknowledged the other bidders' presence.

Sam and Hamdy walked in to the room, nodding to everyone who bothered to look up, as they made their way to the two vacant seats on the front row. Sam carried the envelope given to him by the woman who had visited his home the previous day.

The meeting was about to start.

***

The panel of committee members entered the room and took their places at the allocated tables. Mushka, the secretary, who sat at the far end followed them.

On her entry both Sam and Rubchek looked up. Sam gave her a nod in recognition of the woman with the envelope, she nodded back. Rubchek was more concerned at learning that one of the bidders and Mushka were familiar.

"Ladies and gentlemen, your attention please." the Panel Chairman spoke. "Due to the larger than expected gathering here today, I would ask you, please, to keep your voice levels down so that those who are speaking from the panel can be heard."

Everyone listened attentively, the whirl of the air conditioning fan was suddenly very loud, otherwise had a pin been dropped it would also have been heard.

One of the panel members stood to give an explanation of the proceedings. There would be an introduction, the names of the bidders would be made public, the successful applicant would be named and finally the floor would be opened for general questions.

The time was nearing the final announcement. Both Mr Davies and Mr Gold looked a lot tenser than either Rubchek or Sam. Rubchek was reasonably calm and very confident that knowing his bid was the highest, the offer would be given to him. As far as he was concerned the others may as well have not been there. Sam on the other hand was the most relaxed of all. To him the deal was not the 'be all and end all.' He would be happy with what ever the decision came to.

Mr Davies began to fidget and found trying to keep still an absolute agony. He was banking on winning this deal. His property company had gone public and expanded into Europe at a time when the property markets had taken a dive, as did the shares in the company. The Middle East expansion offered him a way of boosting the value of the shares at the same time. He had already failed to negotiate a Government building contract in Jerusalem and relied on this bid as being the one to keep the company intact and afloat.

Mr Gold had other problems on his mind and was very heavily committed to acquiring this contract. As a lawyer he had been privy to many deals at the embryo stage and a long way from being hatched. He had passed much of the information to a contact in the Stock Exchange and through a private company, of which Mr Gold was a director, he purchased the shares.

Mr Gold had been riding high for a long while until some of his investments dropped dramatically in value leaving him very vulnerable. He was counting on this possible new contract as a lifeline for his family and for his future plans. He had to get the offer.

"And finally ladies and Gentlemen, I would like to announce the successful bid."

All eyes were glued, ears pricked and mouths were gaping.

"The successful bid goes to 'Eilat New Build'."

Some of the onlookers clapped to cheer the decision. Lights flashed from the snapping cameras and the hall seemed to erupt into pandemonium.

Both Mr Gold and Mr Davies bowed their head, in deep disappointment and regret. They were ruined.

"Mr Chairman, Mr Chairman," Sam's voice was smothered in the background. "Mr Chairman, Mr Chairman," he repeated the words again and again, louder and louder, until the room became hushed and all turned to listen.

***

"Mr Chairman, a point of order" Sam raised his voice another decibel.

Even Rubchek stopped in his tracks as every eye focused onto Sam. "I have documents in my position which will show that I have first claim to the land."

All eardrums stretched tighter to take in this new revelation. Sam passed the documents to the Chairman of the committee who immediately opened the fastener and passed the contents among his fellow members.

After a short deliberation and a quick consultation with the lawyer on duty, the chairman turned to the audience. "The documents which have been handed to me do indeed show that on the 16th May 1960 two immigrants from Europe, by the names of Sam Silo and Billy Turner, had put their mark against the centre of the site in question and, by so doing, have the right to first refusal should the site become available for disposal. I, therefore, declare that if Billy's Bar can match the bid, it will automatically be accepted and the offer made to 'Eilat New Build' will be cancelled."

Rubchek sneered from his seat, his face reddening from the rush of angry blood flooding into his head. His eyes glaring with revulsion, he looked at Mushka and realised he had been duped. He stormed out of the room.

Raymond Ross

Chapter 16

The celebrations carried through the night and into the morning, with the entire kibbutz joining in the jubilant triumph. Sam could not believe the way life brought its own surprises and how fate dealt its cards.

"Who would have thought, all those years ago, there was no interest in the area of barren fields next to the coast used by hippies for camping. Then these two ignorant young lads come along and put their name against a spot they intend to pitch their tent. Suddenly it's a legal contract which the authority had to acknowledge." Sam could not sufficiently stress the mind-blowing circumstances of events to Sheba, whilst they danced and drank their delights. "Even with my friend Billy, long time gone, he still looks over us and is probably celebrating in his own way the magic of the day." Sam was getting more and more emotional with every thought of the past.

"Sheba," he stopped dancing. "I forgot. The woman I owe all the gratitude to in the world, the one who discovered the documents, I didn't thank her," Sam leapt to the door. "I must go and find her, give her a hug, no I'll give her a kiss."

"What, at four in the morning!" exclaimed Sheba. "You don't even know where she lives."

"You're right, I'll have to wait till later," agreed Sam. "I'll go and see her tomorrow. She must work for the company who organised the offer. Er, I know they're called Phillips and Sons, based in town. Yes, I'll go tomorrow to thank her.

***

Rubchek arrived at his office, still seething with enormous hatred at being hoodwinked by a nosy parker of a woman. How dare she think she could get the better of him? Who did she think she was and how did she think she was going to get away with it? The pure cheek of her, the pure audacity and impudence of her. No. She would not get away with it. He was going to make her pay.

Rubchek made a telephone call.

***

Mushka had not felt like celebrating. She had seen the blood stained, vampire eyes of Rubchek when the news of the documents came to light. Rubchek's picture horrified her, she was unable to sleep or relax. She could not have known the depth of hatred she had stirred up in a madman's brain.

She paced the room in restless strides until tiredness had taken hold and drugged her to sleep. In her mind the glowing sun shone from the horizon, brightening the day with glowing colours of yellow, brown and amber. Her deep magical dream bounced her from cloud to cloud as she wisped along the gentle breeze.

Her trance would not allow her to hear the white car approach the front entrance to her apartment block, nor did she hear the heavy sledgehammer that ripped the door from its supports. Even the thundering steps on the concrete staircase did not cause her distraction. She was immune to the outside world of fear. Her dream fixed on a single axis with its arrow pointing to a heavenly star.

Her apartment door was the next barrier to suffer a battering, the final obstacle standing in the way of a wonderful and caring woman. Mushka's mind was not awake to the bullet that ruptured her heart nor would it ever wake again.

***

The following day Sam called at the offices of Phillips and Sons to be told of the news that her apartment had been burgled.

"She must have disturbed the thieves. She was shot dead."

From the height of elation, as if standing on Mount Everest viewing the wonders around, he'd been knocked to the burning depths of the devil. Sam was totally flustered by the news like being punched and left flattened in the ring.

He took the news back to Sheba.

***

Rubchek had one more deed to inflict; he had been cheated from what was rightly his. No one crossed his path without suffering the consequences.

He lifted the handset and dialled a number into the telephone.

***

For the second time that day Billy decided to mount his bike and cycle the lap around the kibbutz. He had not managed to beat his record of 18 minutes and 20 seconds. The conditions were just right: not many people to get in the way, the sun was on its downward slope, letting the temperature dip and he felt invigorated and good within. He remembered his birthday chain and swung the Star onto his back so it did not dangle in the way. With the timer set to zero he pressed the signal to start. The clock was ticking. His feet hit both pedals, one up and one down. The cycle took off like a jet propelled by an unwinding elastic band.

He hit the first of the plantation orchards, passing the fruit-laden trees, rode down the little dip and sharply round the 'S' bend, using his feet to scrape the floor in balancing the bike on the tight bend.

Then came the long row of bushes, the tree lined path and the field of vines with the thousands of bees diving at him. He usually sped more quickly at this point so as not to sustain too many stings. Nearing the end of the vineyard he slowed a little to turn right for the old trodden mud path. This path gave him the most trouble. In the past it had cost him many punctured tyres and, on one occasion, a buckled front wheel. That incident was etched in his mind as being the only time his front wheel jammed, sending him flying off into a summersault and on to his back. If he stopped to think about it too long he would remember the terrible pain he suffered.

He was doing well, the timer had clocked ten minutes and there was not far to go, just a few more fields, an open road and then back through the kibbutz to the finishing line.

***

The two men placed a wooden boulder across the road, just where it narrowed at a bend and where a cyclist would not see it until it was too late. They then hid behind some bushes and waited.

***

Billy's leg spun the pedals faster, having reached an area where he could make up time and knock another couple of seconds off.

"Faster!" he shouted to make himself work harder. He raced through the next field and down another track. He knew he would have to take care because he was approaching an area where the roadway narrowed at a bend and it would be hard to stay on the saddle. However, if he was going to beat his record, he would have to maintain his speed, bend or no bend. He continued to thunder along.

Then he saw the wooden boulder across the road. As much as he tried to slow down he was too late and the bike flipped on impact, tossing him in the air to land some yards ahead on his back.

The two men ran out of the bushes, threw a sack over the boy's head and, after tying the end, carried him to their waiting car.

***

Sheba was busy preparing dinner. She wanted to make a special meal in celebration of them having acquired the hotel site. The wine was already in a cooler, the meat soaking in a marinade and the potatoes peeled.

She was a little concerned. Billy had gone on his bike over an hour ago to have another go at beating his lap record. He should have been back.

Dessert was the next item on her mind, the flour to mix and dough to need and finally a pie to make. She preferred apple. Sam liked pear and Billy rhubarb, so on this occasion she was going to mix the lot.

Again she looked out of the window. There was still no sign of Billy.

Having sorted out the food she began to set the table with the cutlery, glasses and serviettes. She put the light on as it was beginning to get dark. The front door opened.

"Billy is that you?" she called.

"No, it's me." Sam walked in.

"Oh Sam. I'm worried. Billy went out on his bike. He's been out ages. Where can he be?"

The telephone rang. Sam answered, his face dropped as he listened.

"We have your son. He'll come to no harm if you do as we say."

"What do you mean you have Billy? What have you done with him? What's going on? What do you mean he'll come to no harm? What have you done with him?" Sam blurted out the questions in a stream of panic, his words terrifying Sheba as she ran over to his side. He turned the earpiece forty-five degrees so that she could listen to the voice on the other end.

"Listen very carefully. Your son is all right. He will come to no harm if you follow our instructions. You must go to the planning office in town and tell them that you have changed your mind. Tell them that you are not going to develop the hotel site after all. Do you understand?" The voice continued. "Ask them to return your bid offer and, as soon as we have confirmation that the site is back on the market, we will release your son."

The telephone went dead.

Both Sam and Sheba were momentarily stunned, bolted to the floor like two rigid posts.

Sheba was the first to stir. "What's happened? Where's Billy? What do they want with him? Sam, Sam, you've got to get him back."

"Sheba, darling," Sam came around. "Calm down. You heard what they said, Billy's OK. We just have to do what they say and he'll be home in no time. They can have the site if it means that much to them."

The telephone rang again. Sam snapped the phone off its cradle.

"Now that you've had a moment to absorb our message," the voice was there again. "let me make sure you understand the situation." The demands were repeated to Sam. "And let me finish by warning you that if you go to the police or try to do anything other than what we have told you, your son's body will be sent to you stuffed in a box. Now tell me you understand," demanded the voice.

"Yes, yes. Please don't let him come to any harm. We don't want the site. You can have it. Just tell me that Billy will be OK."

"I'll put him on but no funny business"

"Dad, Dad I want to go home," Sam's hands clutched tighter as he heard Billy's voice.

"Now tell me again that you understand."

"Yes I do. I do."

"The office opens at 8.00am. Make sure you're there first thing." The line went dead again.

Sam and Sheba stood, their arms wrapped around each other, their heads bent together in grief as the voice's message filtered through their minds. They had the whole evening, the whole night and early morning to go through before they could get Billy back. They had to survive the time.

161

They could not sleep thinking of Billy being held somewhere with strangers probably cold, frightened and hungry. Their minds were in a storm of thoughts as howling-gales pumped through their veins into a reservoir of fright. The night was long, longer than they had ever experienced and the dial they watched on the clock's face would not move.

Would morning ever come?

***

Sam and Sheba lay on the bed, going in and out of a trance, one minute fully awake and the next at the doorway of slumber. Sam's mind was like a spinning top, wobbling as it slowed down and then in balance when it speeded up with a fresh input of despair. Just as his mind wrestled with the next round of spins, a knocking disturbed the rotation. Sam tried to maintain his mind steady, but there it was again, a knocking. Was he dreaming? Was an alien getting in? No, there it was again, this time he woke to hear knocking at the front door.

"Who is it?" He was at the door, the time 1.30 am. He could see a shadowy figure through the glazed doorway.

"I want to help you. I know where Billy is."

Sam opened the door. "What did you say?"

"I know where Billy is."

"Who are you?" enquired Sam in disbelief and with some apprehension as to why this stranger should be at his door in the middle of the night. "How do you know my son?"

"Can I come in?" the stranger continued. "It is very important I speak to you now. We haven't much time if you want Billy back."

162

Sam, a little frightened, opened the door to its full swing and invited the stranger in. He maintained an alert mind should this unfamiliar person be another trick to cause his family more harm.

Sheba had overheard the conversation and hurried to the hallway.

"How do you know my son? How can you help us get him back?" Her words rolled out in fear.

"My name is Gaspov. May I sit down? This must be very difficult for you, but I must tell you everything so that you will understand why we cannot wait. We have to get your son back before morning, or I fear it will be too late." Sam and Sheba listened very thoughtfully.

"Your son has been kidnapped by my boss, Rubchek. He has a casino boat in the centre of the Red Sea, where people gamble and have fun with the ladies, if you know what I mean. Anyway, that's where he is holding Billy."

"We'll phone the police. They'll go out there and get him back," hurried Sam's voice. "Anyway, I'm going to cancel the bid and Billy will be released."

"Not so fast," warned Gaspov. "You are dealing with a ruthless monster. Whatever he says you can be sure he will not do. He does not leave anything to chance; he makes sure that his tracks are always covered. That is why he had my cousin Mushka murdered.

"Mushka, do you mean the lady at the public meeting where the bids were decided?" Sam said in a worried tone.

"Yes, he wanted to know who the bidders were and how much they offered so that he could top their price. She wouldn't tell him, so he had her beaten up until she agreed to give the information. Then when he had all the information Rubchek arranged for her to be killed."

"You are beginning to really scare us," Sheba hurried her words.

"You better had be scared, if you want to get Billy back," he continued. "Rubchek decided that the bids of Mr Gómez from Spain and Mr McGregor from Scotland were too large so, instead of topping their offer, he arranged to murder them. Worse still, he had Mrs Gómez murdered in Spain so that she couldn't report him to the police."

"But the voice on the telephone said that Billy would be released as soon as I cancel my offer." Sam's weak voice leaked out.

"That's what he wants you to believe. He's lying. As soon as you cancel your bid he will have Billy, you and your wife murdered. Trust me he will not let any one of you live."

"What about the police. Can't we get them to board his boat and get Billy?"

"No chance. He's too devious for that. He'll kill Billy the moment the Law comes sniffing and then he'll hunt for you two. After all once you're dead, you won't be building the hotel anyway."

"No. We must act now. We cannot wait until daylight. It will be too late. We must surprise him now, when he believes he has the strongest arm and is ready to celebrate his murderous acts."

"We must board the boat now."

***

The hourly shuttle service, to and from the casino boat, carried gamblers on and off through the night. Gaspov had used the shuttle to come ashore that night, without anyone suspecting him, on the pretence that he was going to a party and meeting a friend.

Sam clothed in a suit, shirt and tie and wearing a large rounded hat mingled with other fortune seekers as he boarded the shuttle for the casino-boat. He tried not to glance in the direction of Gaspov who had boarded some five minutes earlier. Gaspov was busy talking to the boatman, whom he obviously was familiar with and was, no doubt, attempting to make light matter of his journey. In spite of Sam's seemingly cool manner, inside he was suffering from a severe bout of nervousness. He had to be careful: Billy and Sheba were the most important people in his life and he did not want to let them down.

The shuttle reached its destination. Sam nodded thanks to the boatman and proceeded onto the casino boat.

"Good evening Sir, may I take your hat?" The pretty and lightly-clad usherette enquired.

"Thank you, but I would rather keep my hat on. It's a little nippy tonight." Sam's hat offered him some camouflage as did the false moustache he wore.

Gaspov had instructed him well, telling him to mingle in the casino hall for a short while.

"Make your way to one of the women on duty and agree to pay for entertainment. They will lead you into the special parlours located on the bottom deck, very close to where Rubchek will have locked up Billy."

"He has only just been kidnapped and the demands on you are for the morning Rubchek will be feeling very relaxed and pleased with himself. He won't be on guard and probably will be enjoying the company of a woman so this is the perfect opportunity. I'll meet you on the lower deck and together we'll force Billy's door open. You can then make your way, with Billy, to the shuttle boat before Rubchek even knows you are on board."

Sam made his way to the roulette wheel. The table was littered with chips, some piled high on several numbers. Those brave enough to gamble stood round the table clattering their chips, flipping and shuffling them. Some were smiling from their gains whilst others displayed sagging cheeks and drooping eyes from their losses, a contrast between feelings of exaltation and despair. They were all there: the losers, the winners and those just wanting a good time.

"Want to buy a lady a drink?" Sam looked up into the blue eyes of a succulently sexual woman, her dress split hip-high, her long leg tempting his desires as she leaned towards him to reveal the swells of her bosoms. Her sensual lips parted tantalisingly into a circular gap with biting teeth inviting his attention.

"Yes, er, y-yes." Sam stuttered, surprised by her overwhelming power and forwardness. "Er y-yes, what would you like?" he volunteered.

"Champagne would be very nice, over there by the bar." She pointed and wiggled in the same direction. Sam followed, momentarily entranced by her presence before remembering his purpose.

"Actually I'd rather hoped you would take me to your special room. Here, how much do I need to give you?" He waved a few notes at her face.

"Oh, you are a dear one, so rushed and hasty. Well if you can't wait, I'll show you the way," she mused and took the notes from his grasp.

She led him to the doorway. "Let us through, Yentev. I'm entertaining."

Yentev let her lead Sam through the doorway to the stairs. She held his hand, fingers entwined, and took short steps. She was in no hurry, this man had already given her a wad of notes. If she toyed with him a little longer and raised his excitement with extra foreplay he would succumb and be spellbound into parting with more money. She had him by her little finger and he was being escorted like a puppy.

They reached the lower deck and she pulled him towards a row of cabins. Choosing the middle one, they entered.

"So, young man, let's take your hat off and then I promise to make you more comfortable." She pulled him by his tie, curled her lips and rose to him on her toes and, as her mouth came closer, she tantalisingly pulled away. "Let me loosen your shirt." She reached to his belt to undo the buckle.

"Wait, wait." Sam hurried. "I've changed my mind. Here, let me pay you for your time. I'm sorry but I can't go through with this."

Her face turned icy. She covered herself with crossed arms. "OK," she said as she took more notes from Sam and proudly walked out of the cabin, not troubled or concerned at being rejected. She had her money. She was ready for the next punter, whoever he might be.

Sam gave her a few minutes to leave. She had been so engrossed in her own deliberations that she did not realise he was left behind. He carefully opened the cabin door.

***

Gaspov had been sitting by the bar. This being his day off, he was able to casually roam around and use the casino's facilities. He saw Sam from the moment he walked in, making his way around the hall and to the roulette wheel. Sam looked very tense and uneasy, but that was no surprise. This was a very trying moment and a lot depended on their timing.

He then saw Sam walking towards the bar with a lady in hand. They talked for a short while before the two left through the doorway to the staircase. Gaspov waited another five minutes before following them to the lower deck.

As he reached the row of entertainment cabins, the lady who had been with Sam came out of the middle cabin and almost bumped into him. She dashed away towards the staircase whilst he looked for the cabin where Billy was being held. He tried a few doors that opened easily before reaching a secured one which he concluded was Billy's.

He froze for a moment when Sam opened one of the cabin doors to look out.

"Sam," he called out, "over here, I think it's this door."

Sam ran over to Gaspov. They both tried to push the door open but the lock would not budge.

"Billy, can you hear me?" Sam tried to whisper through the door. "Billy, it's Dad. Can you hear me?" There was no answer.

"I can't see it being any other cabin on this deck. I'm sure this is the right one," insisted Gaspov.

"Stand back. I'm going to try my boot," Sam rocked on his left foot sending his right squarely at the door. The lock snapped open. The hinges tore from their screw grips and the door fled from its post.

The two dashed into the cabin. It was empty but for a lonely chair in the middle, a low bunk bed at the side and some discarded litter in the corner. Feeling irritated Gaspov was ready to look elsewhere.

"Wait, what's that?" Sam went to look at the discarded rubbish. He brushed his hand through the bits of paper, sifting all the little pieces through his fingers, when he saw the chain, broken into two strands. His heart choked and faltered a beat. It was Billy's. "Look it's Billy's chain and Star." Excitedly Sam looked up and then he saw the cupboard door.

"What's in there?" Sam forced the door open. It was a little bathroom and on the toilet Billy sat tied, gagged and blindfolded. The two ripped at the thongs, freeing Billy from his nightmare.

"Dad! Dad!" Billy exclaimed wrapping his arms round Sam's neck. His father was with him and he was not letting go. Sam picked him up, hugged and kissed him. Even Gaspov felt an emotional reaction to the reunion.

"It's time to go. Quick, we have to rush," Gaspov kept a sense of order outside the excitement. "Now remember we part here. You must take Billy back upstairs and exit on the shuttle. I'm counting on the fact that Rubchek would have brought Billy here in complete secrecy and placed him downstairs. Just act as if you are a regular customer and walk confidently out. Also, remember Rubchek is not going to like this. He's going to look for you and you've got to get some distance away."

"Come with us. It's going to be dangerous for you to stay aboard."

"No, it's better for me to stay here." Gaspov interrupted. "He doesn't suspect me. He won't have thought anyone brave enough to stand against him and, anyway, my business with him isn't finished. Getting Billy from his clutches is only half way to settling my score with him. The other half is for murdering my cousin, Mushka. I will have her avenged."

Sam and Billy walked carefully and quickly out of the cabin, along the hallway and up the staircase to the doorway leading to the shuttle area.

"Just a minute. Excuse me, Sir." The voice beckoned them to stop. "Excuse me, Sir..." Yentev placed his hand on Sam's shoulder. "Excuse me, Sir." Sam stopped his hurried step to take notice, holding Billy more tightly by the hand so as never to let go.

"Children are not allowed in the casino."

"Oh, yes you're right. I'm taking him home, sorry," Sam continued his pace.

The shuttle set off the minute they boarded.

***

Yentev looked at his watch. It was time to see Rubchek. He walked to the lower deck and before entering Rubchek's cabin, he knocked loudly.

"Enter." Rubchek's command was firm and exact.

169

"Ah, Yentev, how are things upstairs? Have we many guests?"

"It's very busy tonight," Yentev advised. "You wouldn't believe it but one of the guests actually tried to bring a boy on board. Anyway, I saw them off."

"A boy!" shrieked Rubchek who instantly ran to find Billy and on seeing the broken door and no sign of the boy, yelled at Yentev. "Stop the shuttle! Get the motorboat and go after them. Bring them back to me - Now!"

Yentev sprinted the stairs in two's, signalling three of his people to the chase as the motorboat's gears crunched into spin, leaving a wall of the sea's white suds in turmoil.

Sam heard the roaring blades of the craft as it neared the shuttle and realised that they must have been spotted. He could not take the chance.

"Jump Billy. We're going to have to swim for the shore. Jump!"

The two leapt off the shuttle into the icy waters. On surfacing they swam breaststroke to keep the splashes to the minimum, their heads bobbing very gently in the shadows of the narrow smiling moon whose size had shrunk to the smallest crack.

When they reached the shuttle there was no sign of the two runaways. The motorboat made a sweep across the immediate area, gradually widening its arc and displaying its powerful tungsten beams across the rippling seawater. The night was exceptionally dark affording the two swimmers the comfort of its cloak as cover for their escape. On reaching a rocky formation, close to the shore, they were able to take a much-deserved rest from their battle to keep afloat.

The motorboat neared the rocks and for an instance its eyes rested on Billy's head. He dodged to the side. The light followed and then dissipated, assessing it to be a bird disturbed of its sleep. The motorboat rounded again, its crewmembers getting more distressed from their futile search and, as they swung further left, the two swimmers pushed off for the finishing line.

Chapter 17

Rubchek yelled an almighty thunder. His lightning eyes gawked at the three hopeless men who were fidgeting and squirming in absolute terror of his might.

"Twice, twice that devil has slipped away," he boomed. "You idiots. Get out of here. Get off the boat before I feed the lot of you to hungry sharks."

He sat down seething as he did the previous time. Yet again his business had stalled with unfinished work and an eel of a being had slipped his grasp. "He will pay. His wife and child will pay and anyone else who thinks they're brave enough to be his aid."

He picked up the handset and made a long distance phone call.

***

"Sheba, Sheba, quick! Pack your things and put a few items of clothes in a case for Billy." Sam spurted his instructions as he and Billy ran into the house. "We have to get away quickly, before the Russian comes looking for us. He's going to be one mean animal when he discovers Billy's escaped."

Having packed they bundled themselves into a taxi and headed back to Eilat to the Royal Motel situated in the back streets of the town. Sam knew of the motel from the days when he first arrived in Eilat, when he and his pal Billy were foraging for food and work. The motel's manager had been very kind and had given them advice on where to find food and shelter. Sam had had cause to communicate with the manager in more recent times and found him to be reliable and trustworthy.

Another advantage ticked off in Sam's mind for the motel was its location, in a narrow lane and well hidden from busy areas. He was satisfied that Sheba and Billy would be safe whilst he tried to figure out how they were going to remain protected.

***

Ferguson boarded the 07.50 BA flight form Gatwick, London to Amsterdam arriving at 09.50. From there he boarded the El Al flight to Ben Gurian Airport, Tel Aviv, arriving at 17.35, two minutes ahead of schedule and within the time-frame he had set himself for his final destination. He took a taxi to Eilat.

"I recommend plenty of water. Eilat is extremely hot this time of year, with temperatures going over the hundred." The taxi driver tried a little harmless conversation from boredom. "Being at the edge of the desert its like staying in an oven. Have you been to these parts before?"

There was no reply. Ferguson's mind was locked in solitary mode, sharply focused on his task ahead, whose path he travelled in a precise and predetermined manner. For the second time that day he removed an envelope from his inside jacket pocket. The contents: a family photograph, one reservation at the not so popular Sahara Hotel and a wad of currency. He flicked the wad close to his ear and enjoyed recounting the sheets as they floated past.

He rested his back deeper into the cushioned seat and smiled to himself, thinking about the desperate call he received from the Russian. The calls to him always occurred when people were at the end of their tether and this was no different, just as alarming and frantic. To Ferguson this was a relatively easy assignment of carrying out his objectives and then dropping out of sight, leaving no trace.

Another glance at the photograph and he read the labelled names of Sam, Sheba and Billy before replacing the envelope next to his passport. On this occasion he was travelling as Ferguson, a name he had not used for a long time but a lucky one from a previously rewarding assignment.

He closed his eyes. The pawn had hopped two steps allowing both queen and bishop a straight path of attack.

***

The taxi driver dropped his passenger at the Sahara reception area and once registered, Ferguson made his way to his room. He immediately took a shower to energize his travel worn body, to keep it prime and in readiness for all eventualities.

He opened the closet and removed a parcelled box marked for his attention as arranged by Rubchek. The brown wrapping came easily away, as did the lid, to reveal a black leather case with two combination locks for security. He spun the combination until the numbers on both locks exposed the row of figures divulged to him in a previous communication. The locks sprung open and the lid was set free from its secured grip. Ferguson eyes widened in expectation as the automatic gun came into view.

Picking up the lethal weapon, he held it to his cheeks, slid it against his face and paused momentarily to smell the metal in some ritual that stirred his sexual desires. The feel of the barrel gave him the most pleasure, holding it up and rubbing it gently, as he eyed the viewfinder and aimed at a target some metres from where he stood.

Tenderly he placed six bullet cases into the rotating barrel and fearlessly spun it on its axis to establish the ease of balance and speed of performance. The glow in his eyes and the parting grin of his lips were testimonial to his satisfaction. Rubchek had not let him down in providing the handy weapon for implementing his assignment.

White Pawn moves D2 to D4 to stand side by side with Pawn E4 and strengthen his attack. He was ready for his next move.

***

Billy's bar was exceptionally busy, the Chinese and Indian sections fully booked and the European and Mediterranean areas experiencing a very busy turnover of diners. With Hamdy directing the waiters and Magda supervising the kitchen staff meals were quickly prepared and whisked to their intended tables. Sam had made himself available, although he wanted time to think about how he was going to keep his family away from harm. He felt that he would get some extra stimulation from the aura of the place. He directed customers to their tables and helped them journey through the many liquid refreshments listed on the wine menu. The atmosphere was so electric, with a buzz of laughter and regular conversation flying in every direction, as if the whole of Eilat was seated.

Ferguson walked in virtually unnoticed. He sat at the bar and ordered a double scotch. This was a fact-finding mission and he could afford the luxury of alcohol. He spied Sam, his picture engraved in his mind from the family photograph, milling with customers and bobbing from table to table giving assistance. To Ferguson, Sam was just another body, not a person or being, just an object to be terminated and discarded. His target was not an athlete with toned muscles and a stealthy appearance but one with a slight tummy bulge and weak knees. This was going to be easy. He had seen enough, his blazing excitement a little doused by a disappointing challenger. He threw the remaining whisky to the back of his leathery throat, swallowed the fiery liquid and stood to leave.

Sam was scanning the restaurant for anyone wanting assistance, when his attention pointed at a man walking from the bar. His brain juggled with flashing images of the past and enquired of itself if had it seen this man before? The historical imagery data processed in nanoseconds through his soft brain tissues, building a jigsaw picture until it was complete. Sam remembered. It was the hit man on the cargo ship that took him across the Mediterranean all those years ago.

Sam was bewildered at this chance meeting and tried to make sense of it, asking himself was it coincidental or was the man there for a purpose. Why was there a hit man at his restaurant? There was no logic until Sam thought of Rubchek and then the whole picture fell together. The man could not have remembered the sight of a young lad, now grown up into an adult with completely changed features. A change which is dramatic from teenage to adulthood but less so from young adulthood to middle age.

"Hamdy, quick," Sam called him. "Hamdy, quickly, take off your overall. Do you see that man walking by the bar towards the exit door?" Hamdy nodded his answer. "Follow him. I want to know where he's going, what he's doing here and where he's staying." Hamdy followed the man out of the bar.

***

Ferguson drove his rented car to Kibbutz Eilot. He did not notice Hamdy following from a good distance. He arrived at Sam's house and circled the area a couple of times before coming to a stop. He walked to the front door. There was no answer to the bell. He tried round the back but no one was at home. Feeling a little disappointed he called on a neighbour.

"They're away for a few days. Who should I say called?"

"I'm Dr Duncan, from England, sorry to disturb you but I'm looking for Sheba. I have some important news for her. Do you know where she may have gone?"

"Sorry no, but you might try her mother Dr Shoshana Goodman at the hospital in town," offered the neighbour.

"Thank you, I will." Ferguson returned to his car and drove back to town.

Hamdy continued to follow.

***

"Magda, will you look after the restaurant? I need to get back to Sheba with an urgent matter."

"Of course, don't worry, Sam. As the tourists say: 'running this place is as easy as pie.' Take your time I'm here till the last drink is served." Magda sent Sam on his way.

Sam hurried to Sheba and Billy, worried for their safety and cautious not to be followed.

***

"I'm looking for Dr Goodman," Ferguson spoke to the receptionist at the desk.

"Just a moment, please," the receptionist looked at her timetable. "I'm sorry, she's in surgery and can't be disturbed. If you would like to leave a message, I'll make sure she gets it."

"I'm Dr Duncan from England. I have some news for her. Would you mind if I waited and may I use the bathroom?"

"Yes, of course, it's along the hallway on the right."

Ferguson stepped down the hall, past the toilet signs and continued to the door marked Staff Only. He entered a long corridor from which wards branched left and right and then sighted a storeroom where he was able to don a white medical gown. From his pocket he removed a badge and placed his business card inside with the name Dr Duncan. He attached the badge to the gown and proceeded to walk along the corridor.

Nurses and patients passed him without giving him another glance; to them he was just another medic attending to his work.

He found the doctor's locker room and went to each locker, reading the door names until he reached Dr Shoshana Goodman. It was locked. From the set of tool keys he carried he drew out the one that seemed the most suitable and began prising the lock. He tried another and another until one fit snugly. The lock opened. Inside Shoshana's clothes hung on a peg. He searched through her jacket pocket and her coat. There was nothing. Then he saw her handbag. He poured the contents on the floor: a purse, a lipstick, some other make-up sticks, tissues, keys and then he spotted a piece of paper inscribed with the 'Royal Motel'.

Ferguson left the hospital, driving left into the main road. Hamdy followed at a distance.

***

Sam entered the Royal and took the staircase three at a time. He had to hurry. There was no time for the lift to stop at each floor because of a mechanical fault.

He found Sheba and Billy playing cards on the balcony.

"I could be wrong, but it seems very odd. I just recognised a man at the restaurant, someone dangerous from a long time ago." Sam reeled off his warning. "I think Rubchek sent him to look for us." Sam proceeded to describe the man, his height, clothing, appearance and colour. "Just keep your eyes glued whenever you're out."

"Sam, this is ridiculous. A monster is hunting us and now there's probably a contract on our lives. We can't carry on like this. You must go to the police. We need their help." Sheba released her terrified feelings. She and Billy just could not continue to live like victims on the run.

Sam promised to go to the authorities, but first he had to find Hamdy.

***

Ferguson checked his tourist street map and came to a halt a few side streets from the Royal. He reached for his side holster, took out the automatic and gave the barrel a quick spin before placing it back. He was ready, his nose almost sniffing his prey.

Queen D1 to D3, he was winding the springs of attack.

Ferguson walked the few hundred metres to the Royal. He stood outside for a moment to take in the layout of the exterior structure. The main entrance in the middle was flanked by bedrooms, their balconies jutting out on all seven floors and tiered outwards with the bottom balcony standing out the furthest.

Sheba spotted him standing at the corner. He looked up. Their eyes momentarily locked before she dragged Billy inside.

Ferguson hurried inside taking to the stairs. The element of surprise was gone. There was a need for urgency. The gun was already out of its resting place and in his grip, pointing his path. Up the first, second, third and fourth flight his legs, cushioned by their muscular structure, cracked the stoned floor as they battled up.

Sheba tugged at Billy. They both scurried like frightened hares being pursued by a pack of hungry hounds. They reached the far end of the hall where the emergency door stood guard to the outer fire escape. Their propelled bodies crashed against the fire door's cross bar, exerting their latent energies to force it open. They had reached the outside metal stair escape.

Ferguson thundered through the fourth floor doorway into the hall area and began to systematically shoot open a number of bedroom doors in his search. One was ajar. He rushed in and searched the en suite and the balcony. They were gone. He dived back into the hallway and sighted the emergency exit door still swinging from its previous attackers. He ran towards the exit.

Billy raced ahead of Sheba, his legs thrusting him faster and on reaching the bottom he looked up. "Quick, Mum! Faster, he's catching up."

Sheba landed against Billy, the two tumbling for a moment before getting up and racing round the corner.

Ferguson's body heaved onto the fire stair as his momentum guided him downwards. They had been out of sight but he figured they could only be metres away from him, perhaps round the next corner or two. Onwards he motored, in top gear, sending his charged energies to all the extremes of his muscles.

The two fled round one corner then another and another, before spying a taxi and yanking the doors open in shouts of, "Go, go, go!" The driver shocked from his newspaper reflexed the car forward before he had time to realise what was going on.

Ferguson was left ranting at the pavement side in anger at their escape.

Queen D3 back to D1 to regroup.

Hamdy followed Ferguson to the Sahara hotel.

Chapter 18

"Mr Ferguson?" the telephonist enquired.

"Yes," Ferguson answered having picked up the receiver.

"I have a call for you," and without waiting a reply put the caller through.

"This is a message from Rubchek. Mother and son are staying at the hospital." The telephone went dead.

Frantically and in temper he punched the telephone cradle buttons up and down until the receptionist answered. "Reception, can I help you?"

"Who did you just put through to my number?" Ferguson demanded.

"Sorry, Sir. I didn't take his name. I thought you knew him. He was very friendly and seemed to know you well. Is there anything else I can help you with, Sir?"

Ferguson slammed down the receiver in annoyance. He was not familiar with the unpredictable. Everything he did he calculated and exercised in total control. He was the master and administrator, one of the same in perfect harmony with his objectives. Not knowing who the caller was niggled his senses and made the hairs on the nape of his neck stand up and shiver.

The two had escaped him. They will not escape again. He reloaded his automatic and gave it a spin before placing it into its clasp.

Ferguson took a taxi to the hospital.

Queen D1 back to D3; he was in control again.

***

"Dr Duncan to see Dr Goodman," Ferguson announced to the receptionist as a matter of urgency. She looked up from her file. It was the same receptionist as on his previous visit.

"Ah, yes, Dr Duncan. Let me see. She's doing her rounds at the moment and should be free in an hour," she replied having consulted her daily schedule sheet.

"That's alright. I'm actually here to see her daughter and grandchild, Sheba and Billy," he continued. "I have some wonderful news for them and I'm very anxious to see them. Should I go through to the staff accommodation unit?" He took her by surprise, as if he was not meant to know and was confirming his information.

"Oh, er, they're not here," she flustered. Now he was positive she was lying.

"Thank you, you say an hour? That's fine. I'll call back," and he was gone.

Ferguson walked round to the back of the hospital, to the service entrance where a number of lorries were in the process of being off-loaded. He picked up one of the boxes, put it against his shoulder and easily slipped into the hospital undetected. Passing through the loading bay and goods-in office, he placed the parcel onto one of the pallets supporting other boxes and proceeded further into the building.

The accommodation unit was located at the furthest end of the building from where he had entered and he preferred to be less conspicuous. He entered the laundry area.

"Can I help you?" the lady in charge offered her assistance.

"Yes please, I'm Doctor Duncan. I'm here as a locum. Doctor Goodman asked me to robe in whites whilst I'm on duty. Do you have my size?"

"Oh yes, here you go. This should fit you. Actually all the male fittings are the same, you just have to adjust the belt," she mused.

"Thank you."

In a white robe he felt a lot more comfortable and more camouflaged, facilitating his purpose and final goal. He continued past the x-ray department, the blood clinic, the orthopaedic and intensive wards and finally arrived at double mahogany polished doors marked 'accommodation'.

He entered the area and slowly moved from door to door, listening for any sign of occupation. He figured the place would be deserted, as everyone would be busy with regular hospital business, apart from Sheba and Billy. If they were in the building they would be hiding here, thinking they would be safe.

He continued looking and, as he moved forward, sounds of a television station grew more audible. Slowly, he crept forward, his automatic balanced in the right hand while the left brushed against the wall to keep in balance with his steps.

Nearing the TV room he could make out that the occupants were watching a comedy show, giggling and laughing with the show cast as the hilarious scenes unfolded. This was going to be easy. They would be too engrossed to either notice him coming in or feel the bullets rip through their flesh. He smiled and beamed in great expectation.

He slowly swivelled the door handle and guided his feet inside. They were sitting on the settee, legs supported by a stool, in relaxed mode happily being entertained.

Bishop F1 to H3, Pawn E4 to E5.

He felt a massive burst of power surge through him as he lifted the automatic to take aim.

***

"Ferguson put the gun down. We have you surrounded." He stood his ground, slowly turning his head. From the left, two police officers came out of the adjoining door, from behind, another officer and another to the right and finally two from the bathroom area ahead. He was surrounded. There was no way out. It was a trap and he had fallen straight into their hands.

He slowly lowered the gun, turning it ninety degrees to point in his direction. The barrel exploded. The bullet tore through his head.

White King cedes. Check Mate.

***

Rubchek sat at his desk, deflated by the news that Ferguson had failed with his mission and that Sam had once again slipped out of his grasp. He thumped his annoyance on the wooden desk, causing the strained timber to crack and as he readied for another thump the cabin door opened.

"Who said you could come in?"

The man entered the room, slowly pacing towards Rubchek and as he neared he held his gun up and pointed.

"You don't frighten me. You're a weak and a pathetic coward, just like your relative. Now get out, before I kick you out." Rubchek snarled his gritted teeth at him.

The man pulled back the hammerhead, his hands shaking as his finger juggled with the trigger.

"Coward. Go on. Get out, coward," echoed Rubchek's words.

The man moved closer. He was shaking uncontrollably.

"Just look at you. You're pathetic. You're shaking like the sails of the ship." Rubchek placed his right hand under the desk and from a secret shelf took hold of a small gun. He pointed it at the man and fired. The bullet exploded out of its chamber, pierced the back of the desk and soared at the man. It ripped through the man's baggy shirt and nicked the side of his upper body before lodging itself into the wooden wall of the cabin. The man fell backwards from the shock.

Rubchek rose from his seat and walked to the front of his desk. The man recovered from the fall and in spite of a little trickle of blood was able to get up.

"You may as well stay down like the idiot you are." Rubchek moved forward in readiness to fire again. The man charged with his gun at Rubchek and as he thudded at him the two tumbled over. Both guns fired their round with one bullet careering wide and out of control whilst the other tore through its intended target.

The two men were locked together, with one lying on top of the other. Rubchek eyes opened wide, his grin turning into a broad smile and as his heart stopped beating his muscles locked their stance.

Gaspov rose from the floor. He threw the wasted gun to the side and as he left the cabin, thinking of Mushka, he looked towards the heavens and said, "You can now rest in peace."

***

The police officer congratulated Sam for his quick thinking mind.

Sam in turn thanked the police for helping him snare Ferguson at the hospital. Having learnt from Hamdy that Ferguson was staying at the Sahara Hotel, he telephoned with a bogus message from Rubchek that Sheba and Billy had run to the hospital for shelter. From then on it was only a matter of time before Ferguson concluded his own demise.

Sam also gave detailed information to the police of Rubchek's crooked business dealings and the death contracts he had initiated. Although the police were unable to board the boat, it being anchored outside their jurisdiction, they were a little surprised to see it sail out of the Red Sea without any fuss.

Chapter 19

Sam, Sheba and Billy were jubilant in being able to return to some normality, the threat on their lives being lifted and freedom once more part of their lives. Not having to look behind their backs was a luxury they had nearly forgotten and were very pleased to regain.

Billy looked at the future. He had great expectations and hopes of achievement and, having acquired the lease for the land by the coastal waters of the Red Sea, the way ahead pointed to prosperous and thriving times.

He had a plan and was ready to share it with the world but first he had to see Gaspov.

***

He guessed right when he found Gaspov living in Mushka's apartment.

"I thought I'd find you here." Gaspov was pleased to see Sam. "I suppose you haven't a job?" Gaspov shook his head. "No money," he shook his head again. "No food and nowhere to go. Well Gaspov I want you to be my partner. I have great plans for our future and I need you to help me see them through. What do you say?"

Gaspov was speechless, but managed to mumble, "Yes." Minutes later he was energized and ready for whatever Sam had in mind.

"Right, now let's contact the following people, we need to meet them on the site of our new hotel and we need to meet them quickly."

***

They had all come, their curiosity well sharpened, their expectations in full bloom and blossoming all the while, questions at the tip of their tongues, frustrated with the lack of answers.

The meeting was about to begin. Sam stood in the centre of the semi-circle of chairs where each guest sat. Gaspov had organised a small marquee to be erected on the site as well as a seating area and refreshments for everyone to tuck into.

Sitting next to Sam were Sheba and Billy, together with Shoshana and Jack. He wanted all his family with him on this momentous occasion.

"Thank you all for coming," Sam began. "I know that some of you have travelled many miles, but what I have to offer you today will be for ever a monumental tower for a dear lost soul. You have all suffered a common loss and I intend to unite with you in achieving greatness from this present disaster."

"Bids were invited for the purchase of the lease to this site, with planning permission for a great hotel. Eilat will become the focus of every travel company in the world over the next few years. It will be the most important destination for tourists and will generate enormous wealth."

"Your loved ones had realised the potential of acquiring this site and had tended a fair bid and in so doing became the targets of greed and malice. Each of you has lost a dear relative through the hands of a murderous individual."

Sam paused for a moment, reflecting on the toll of deceased: Marvin Goldman and his secretary Nancy, Arthur McGregor, Carlos Gómez and his wife Carolina, and finally Mushka.

Inviting the families of the deceased was a brain wave of his as he needed investors to progress with his goal of building a grand hotel on the shores of the Red Sea. The families gathered before him had already made their intentions of investment known, through those who were murdered. He had also invited to the meeting the two unsuccessful bidders, Robert Davies and Moshe Gold.

Sam walked over to a table at the corner of the marquee. On the table was a large object covered in a white cloth. He took hold of one corner and pulled the cloth away, like a magician sweeping the tablecloth without disturbing the china.

"Ladies and gentlemen," Sam continued, "welcome to 'The Grand Sheba Hotel'." He paused to let the image sink in, of a wooden model depicting the dynamic structure.

"The Grand Sheba Hotel will be the most prestigious and modern hotel in Eilat and will tower above the skyline of the town. It will be constructed with the finest building materials available, marble flooring and exquisite furnishing. It will become known throughout the world as the most sought after destination." He walked to Sheba and took hold of her hand, "named after my beautiful wife." He gave her a kiss.

"I would like to offer each of you a partnership in building the grandest hotel on these shores. With our financial power we will build, not only one hotel, but a string of hotels throughout the world."

"Come," he waved them over, "have a closer look, this is your future."

189

Gaspov poured champagne and handed a glass to each person.

"A toast: to the future of the Grand Sheba Hotel." They all toasted as, one by one, they signed a partnership agreement.

No one took notice of the extra site tagged alongside the hotel model. If they had, Sam would have said.

"This is the second part of my news."

Chapter 20

So began the construction of The Grand Sheba Hotel. Sam brought together the finest architects. He wanted imagination and forward thinking and he wanted plans that would determine the way all future hotels were constructed. It would be a show-palace for all to replicate.

He met with interior designers and analysed their ideas, playing one against the other in his aim of achieving an interior look that would be awesome to the eye. Sam wanted guests to marvel at the spectacle of their entry to the hotel and to feel a sensual experience in the enclosed warmth of its body.

He employed a public relations company to present regular bulletins of progress and to build strong bridges with all agencies involved with the travel industry. Their task: to fire up curiosity and interest, to hype up a sheer excitement and to get people talking and gossiping about the Eilat of the future.

Newspapers and periodicals, broadcasting agencies and television and radio companies were invited to further manipulate people's thoughts and to spotlight the birth of a new and exciting hotel experience.

"Sheba, I want to show you something," Sam requested.

"What?" she responded.

"I'll tell you when we get there," was all he was willing to say.

They travelled by car up a winding hilly track, where the mountains of the desert stood in their spectrum colours of browns and golds and, on reaching the peak, Sam pulled over. He took Sheba by the hand.

"Close your eyes. I have a surprise for you." He led her to the edge of a protruding ridge and placed her facing east. "Now open them. On focusing her pupils she melted from the joy of seeing a wondrous structure towering above the skyline of Eilat. Across the structure she could read 'The Grand Sheba Hotel'.

"Come on, I want you to be the first to walk in". They raced back and, as they neared the hotel, its colossal mass and gigantic height and width extended well beyond the focal point of their eyes. They drove into the grounds, up the slight incline of the pathway lined with palm trees, edged with grassy embankments and decorated with sprinkling fountains.

A huge canopy structure, glittering with glassy stones in a mass of bright colours, semi circled the entrance to the lobby where rotating glass doors guarded by marble pillars tantalised with their inviting powers.

On entering the huge Reception Lobby, the floor blanketed in best Italian Carrera Marble sweeping in shades of pinks and climbing columns in greys, the two gawked at the many features of lavish wonder. The ceilings supported sculptured figurines depicting fantasies and dreams of magic eras of heraldry. Large window features panelled in stainless steel lined two of the high-rise walls reflecting the dazzle of chandeliers chained to hang low and bewilderingly.

They stopped at the winding staircase, guarded by balusters, as it arched upwards in white-veined marble steps. Alongside they entered one of the six windowed lifts to be elevated, without resistance and in swift momentum, to the top opulent suites.

The rooms were of marbled floors layered with Arabian carpets, the furniture in polished mahogany with gold handles and edgings, and from

192

the walls hung original works of floral art giving an air of warmth and uniqueness.

"Now, come and look at the view." Sam guided Sheba through the glazed patio doors and, as they stood together on the balcony, the mass of the Red Sea bobbed ahead with its litter of boats powering white foam in their wake as they skimmed its surface. The panoramic view was more amazing than any they had witnessed previously.

"It's so beautiful here." Sheba snuggled nearer to Sam, her head resting under his chin and into the folds of his neck, so happy in admiration of his achievements.

"No time for cuddling, I want to show you something else."

They stopped on the mezzanine floor, its window walls tinted from the glow of the sun throwing multicoloured blue and red shadows in its presence. Sam led her through the large automatic swing doors and onto the staircase floating down to the overstocked gardens and swimming pool areas. Flower borders and evergreen shrubs cascaded the leisure and sunbathing quarters.

"Look," Sam pointed towards one of the three swimming pools, "over there, can you see the sign?"

She could. She turned to him for a hug, and she knew the fondness and kindness which permeated his whole being, always thinking of others before himself. Looking again she read the sign. "Billy's Bar."

***

The big band tuned their trumpets. The fuse to the fireworks' display had been made ready to light, the streamers held in readiness to throw and the poppers held taut for explosion.

"Ten, nine, eight," the countdown had begun with the loudspeaker echoing the seconds, "three, two, one. Welcome to the Grand Sheba Hotel." All speakers thundered the message as the band struck a crescendo of sounds and the day exploded into fireworks, crackers, poppers and streamers. The people had come in numbers to witness the opening and join in the pageantry of the occasion.

Films and television celebrities came in their glittering diamonds and designer outfits, some for the media exposure, whilst others came because they genuinely felt the magnetism of the place.

Rooms and suites were fully booked for months ahead and reservations extended well into the following two years. Everyone wanted to be part of the atmosphere the hotel had generated and this was where they wanted to bring their families to holiday.

The following day the press headlined the Grand Sheba Hotel with illustrations of the party atmosphere and messages of good luck and kind wishes for the future. It reported on the futuristic and dazzling look of the complex and likened it to one of the wonders of the world.

Sam released news of his expansion programme. He wanted similar hotels in the French Riviera, Costa del Sol and Florida before embarking on the capitals of the world.

***

The front page of the local newspaper reported on a suicide bombing attack with a number of deaths and many casualties. Two terorists had deguised themselveas members of a religious sect and had entered a public building, blowing themselves up as well as many cevilians.

Chapter 21

"Gaspov, it's time to have another meeting with our partners." Sam was ready to impart the next phase of his plan.

***

On this occasion the invited guests were seated in the plush surroundings of the boardroom suit of the Grand Sheba Hotel. Behind them and fixed to the wall were photographs of those family members who were victims to the procurement of the hotel site. Sandwiches and drinks had been served and the partners were eagerly waiting for Sam to speak.

"Congratulations," Sam raised his glass to everyone. "To the Partnership and the future." They all joined in the toast.

"Our share values have rapidly risen into the best 100 performers of the London Stock Market. We've enjoyed windfall returns on dividends and have reached a business level well beyond many of our expectations. So, my friends, now is the time to take the business to the next dimension."

Sam held a plant for everyone to see. "For those who don't know, this is an Aloe Vera plant. It grows to about 60 to 90 centimetres in height and has plump leaves of 40 to 50 centimetres in length. But what is important is it grows wildly and aggressively in the Israeli climate. Now I want to show you its magical properties."

Sam took a firm hold of one of the leaves and snapped it off at the base. He then took a knife and sliced across the centre of the leaf to allow the sap to leak out onto a plate.

"Now, I want you all to dip your fingers into the sap and to rub the liquid onto any part of your body."

One by one they followed his instructions, some taking a fairly large dollop and spreading it over a wide area of skin whilst others were more sceptical and only slightly dipped into the sap and barely placed it onto themselves.

"Is that a recent cut?"

"Yes," came the reply.

Sam noticed one of the members with a plaster on one finger. "Would you mind if I removed the plaster? I'd like you to put some of the Aloe Vera pulp on the wound, see if it makes any difference." The member agreed

The room seemed to elevate from the increased happy reaction of those who had spread a sizable amount of the liquid. Their favourable response had them in a trance of wonderment and exhilaration from the experience of Aloe Vera.

"This sap or gel, whatever you care to call it, has a wonderful healing properties." Sam began to explain the power that had ignited his feelings for the product. "Apart from making the skin feel smooth and soft, it is an excellent healer of things like burns, stings and minor cuts. Can you imagine? If we contain the gel in the form of a cream we would be able to market it. Not only for first-aid purposes but also women could use it as a rejuvenating cream, and in shampoos and hair lotions. The possibilities are enormous but there's one thing for sure; the product is sensational for marketing."

"How's the wound?"

"It feels a lot better. Can I take one of the leaves for later?

"Of course." Sam was pleased to have proven his point.

Sam was not finished, now for the coup de grâce.

***

He held up a bucket of Dead Sea Mud.

Gaspov took his cue and invited a female model into the room. The partners gaped as the mud was spread over the model's face and with a lamp allowed to dry.

"You may not believe this, but there are people who come from all over the world every year to the Dead Sea, in order to put this mud all over their bodies." He let them gawp a little longer.

"This mud has the properties of making you feel full of energy and younger, by relaxing your tensions and soothing pains. People swear by its healing powers through it increasing blood circulation and metabolic rate. If applied to painful areas it can bring relief and comfort. Rheumatism and backache sufferers can benefit, as can those suffering with skin ailments such as eczema."

"So what does all this mean to us as a partnership?"

Sam walked to the table at the side and pointed at the original model of the hotel. "When you first looked at this model, five years ago, you may not have noticed the site adjoining the hotel. Well I invested some of the company's funds into its purchase. What I would like to do is recommend that we build a beauty centre next to the hotel. Instead of our customers going to it, let us bring the Dead Sea mud and the Aloe Vera gel to them and let them benefit from our service in the comfort of a beauty clinic."

Gasps of excitement filtered throughout the room, each partner mesmerised by Sam's words, as if held in a meditative trance.

"Let me continue." They came out of his spell.

"Why stop with a clinic in Eilat? We can open, through a franchise company, beauty clinics in every country and in every city. The opportunity is unlimited. We will have the power to bring health to the doorsteps of the public without them having to book expensive holidays in faraway destinations."

A sudden round of applause shadowed his words as they rose to give him a standing ovation to such a scheme.

Sam did not need a vote. The applause said everything.

Chapter 22

The Israeli Newspaper business section featured Sam's photograph together with the remaining board of directors, with headlines of 'Local company spreads its wings all over the world'. The article focused on ten new hotel developments and over fifty franchised beauty clinics in many of the European countries and America.

The company was quoted in the London Stock Exchange as being in the top twenty of their best performers.

The front page of the paper reported the suicidal terrorist bomb attack on the number 5 bus on Dizengoff Street in Tel-Aviv. Twenty-one Israelis and one Dutch national were killed. The year was 1994.

***

The following years were the best for Sam, enjoying life with Sheba, seeing Billy grow into an adult, and spending time with Shoshana and Jack. The growth of the company required him to travel regularly from home but, when the opportunity to spend more time with his family was available, he relished the days, like a child with his toys.

"We've been invited to a bar mitzvah," Sheba mentioned one day when the two were peacefully sitting on their porch, enjoying a rare bit of relaxed time together. Sam had a business book in hand and Sheba was engrossed in a novel.

"Remember my cousin Lea in Jerusalem? Her son is approaching 13 years of age; I think the date is in April. Do you reckon we could all go? I haven't seen them for many years and anyway it would a good time to be together and a few days touring the region would be nice."

"Yes, let's do it," he lowered his book and pushed his seat closer, "but first you're going to have to give me a kiss or the deal's off."

"Well if that's all it takes," she reached over for a peck.

"Oh, no you don't," he grabbed hold of her. "you don't get away with it that easy. Now come here."

She easily gave in to his command. Their lips met as she nestled into his powerful arms, the power he would need to preserve for the difficult years ahead.

***

April arrived as quickly as the years had disappeared. All five helicoptered to Jerusalem, courtesy of the Hilton Hotel, the pilot, Shoshana and Jack at the front and Sam, Sheba and Billy in the back.

The smooth flight was in total contrast to the rugged mountain terrain of the desert below them, which afforded a wonderful view of the dangers that lurked in its make-up.

As the helicopter hovered reflections of the same trail caught Sam's attention when he and Sheba had journeyed on their honeymoon. They also followed the path northwards along the Arava Valley, through Sodom, Ein Gedi and Masada.

Nearing Jerusalem the helicopter angled northwest over the Judean Desert, Hebron and Bethlehem, the birthplace of King David and a thousand years later of Jesus. Sam's knowledge of the historical and biblical eras were rather limited but he did enjoy listening to Sheba's explanations of the hive of activity that embraced the pinpoint area of such a tiny but significant part of the world.

The helicopter swooped over Jerusalem, a sight of overwhelming magnificence, tinted in tones of amber and gold. The surrounding peaks with their apartment settlements guarded the central town with buildings depicted white, grey and yellowy brown.

High-rise buildings grew to enormous heights displaying their modern architectural beauty and their compatibility in standing shoulder-to-shoulder with the ancient.

The helicopter homed towards its target like a thrown dart hitting the bull's eye, as it came to rest on the centre circle of the landing pad. The party was greeted by the smiling hotel staff and shown to their VIP rooms, suites kept for very important guests and they included Sam and his party as respected competitors.

They had purposely arrived three days early for the bar mitzvah in order to spend a couple of days touring the Old and New Cities of Jerusalem. This was a luxury they had spoken about many times and yet it had been delayed through periods of difficulties and demanding work schedules.

No sooner had they rested than they walked the streets of the Old City, with Sam and Sheba hand in hand like children, Billy keeping a few feet away looking grown up and Shoshana and Jack trailing behind and trying to keep in contact with the leaders.

Sam merrily snapped his camera as they followed the route through the Christian, Muslim and the Jewish Quarters to the Western Wall where many Jews gathered daily for prayers. The men were at one end, women at the other, each happily displaying their religious obligations with pride.

Sam scribbled a note and placed it into 'God's Letter Box' between the small gaps of the brickwork and wherever a piece of paper could be wedged.

***

He spread the black jacket, black trousers and white shirt neatly across the seat of the chair alongside the broad and black circular hat. The black polished and laced shoes stood at the foot. He smiled, thinking about the many days of preparation and he looked in the mirror at his longer than usual beard, and his long and dangling side burns. His scorn intensified knowing that, although he hated his image, he had to wear it in disguise of his motives.

He felt the rise of his pure hatred pumping his blood vessels and pointing him to martyrdom and the ultimate roots of his beliefs. He was ready but the night would be long.

***

The following day they decided to proceed along the New City, with Sam snapping more photographs they walked up the Mount of Olives where Jesus was said to have made his entrance into Jerusalem. Being over one hundred metres higher than the old city provided them a wonderful view at the top.

They then followed the road to the Israeli Parliament, the Knesset. Finally they took the route to Yad Vashem, the national monument recalling the extermination of six million European Jews under the Nazi regime. Sam took hold of Sheba and she held onto Billy as they walked solemnly through the semi-darkness of the Hall of Remembrance where the names of the main concentration and extermination camps are engraved.

"I feel a little peckish," announced Billy. "Can we stop for a while? My feet are killing me and I'm fed up looking at buildings."

***

He boarded the bus to Jerusalem. No one seemed to pay any attention to him in his attire. From the outside he looked just like any other religious Jewish student, dressed in black and with white tassels hanging from behind his jacket, almost to his knees.

From the inside he was primed like the end of a fuse, wired and ready to be lit. Thoughts of his family inspired him to succeed in his endeavour, right until the end and beyond.

The bus reached its destination. He alighted and walked proudly to his target.

***

Sam and Jack were busy reading the names of the concentration camps and studying their geographical areas in relation to the centre of Germany and the outer lying European countries.

"Sam, Billy's fed up," called Sheba, "he's hungry and I think we should start to head back." Shoshana and Jack decided to go back to the hotel whilst the others opted for the bars and cafés of Ben Yehuda Street in the centre of Jerusalem's busy shopping complex.

A short taxi ride and they were back amongst thousands of people:

shoppers, workers, business people and tourists. They found Ben Yehuda Street and entered one of the cafes.

They sat peacefully at a central table, resting and happy in their thoughts: Billy looking at leaflets he had collected, Sam eyeing Sheba in the sparkle that had first attracted their attention in Billy's Bar so many years ago. The sparkle had grown more intense with age and as she eyed him back, with equal affection. In a glorious moonbeam of happiness and love they continued to hold the moment, not daring to back away.

"I love you," her lips signalled the words.

"I love you," he signalled back.

***

He walked along the paved shopping parade, brushing against the many shoppers who were busy going about their own business. His heart beat faster. He was tense and tight-muscled as he turned into Ben Yehuda Street.

He entered the café.

***

"There's a camera shop nearby. Order me a sandwich and soda. I'll be back in a moment. I just want to get another roll of film for this afternoon," Sam announced as he exited, bumping into a very edgy looking man who stood in the middle, no doubt looking for an empty seat.

Sam walked into the camera shop. The explosion behind him was deafening.

Raymond Ross

Chapter 23

"Last call for passengers flying with El Al to London, please make your way to boarding gate 35," the public tannoy sounded.

Sam was already seated in business class. He rested his head back onto the cushion and closed his eyes to reflect on the three weeks following the explosion and as he did so, he wiped away the drops of tears seeping through his tangled eyelashes. No amount of tranquillisers could smother the devastation that he had witnessed but not been part of. He had seen his beloved snatched away by some mad terrorist and militant extremist.

There were only a few casualties. The bomb had been detonated from the centre of the café giving no chance of survival to anyone within its immediate reach. Any mercy that could be summoned from the disaster was the knowledge that those who died would not have felt any pain nor known of their demise.

The shock of such a disaster weighed heavily on his mind. He could not erase the horrific sight of mangled bodies and torn limbs. Nor could he blow away the smell of the carnage that had lodged itself in the lining of his nasal passages.

The family had been very good to him, with messages of sympathy, love and understanding. Even when he sat with Shoshana during the week of mourning, the many friends and relatives who visited could not have done more in their willingness to open their hearts for the bereaved.

Guilt had invaded his entire body, with so many unanswered questions: why did he not stay in the café? Why did he not look after his family? Why did they choose that particular café when there were so many others? The questions rolled on and on like a Ferris wheel spinning faster with each turn.

He had come as a young man to Israel. Now the country that had given him material wealth had taken away his soul.

The plane took off, the wheels tucking themselves into their compartments as the left wing dipped to curve the flight westwards across the Mediterranean.

Sam looked down. The flight path took him over the tallest building in view, lit up as 'The Grand Sheba Hotel.' As he read the name, images of his beloved Sheba came blooming into his mind, like a rose with a beautiful face at the end of a long stalk. He could feel her touch, with petals so soft and smelling of sweet scents. It reminded him of the feathery pillow she used at night. The one she would nestle into and, when they made love, her aroma would spill onto its cotton case. He loved to bring it against his face, to feel its softness and smell her presence. Oh, how he missed her. She was gone. How would he ever survive her absence?

And, as the plane flew further over the Grand Sheba hotel, he glimpsed alongside, a single-story restaurant illuminated with the name 'Billy's Bar'. He held on to the name momentarily and then took a deep breath letting the air filter through the depths of his lungs. He closed his eyes and relaxed against the headrest before releasing the stream of used air from within, fully spent and ready to be re-oxidised.

He turned to the seat next to him and took hold of Billy's hand. "To think, Mum sent you to tell me we also needed batteries. Her instincts gave you life and took away hers."

Her memory would stay with him throughout eternity.

"Where to?" Sam enquired.

"To Liverpool; I want to see where you were born."

Sam leaned over and gave him a hug before wiping away another tear.

Raymond Ross

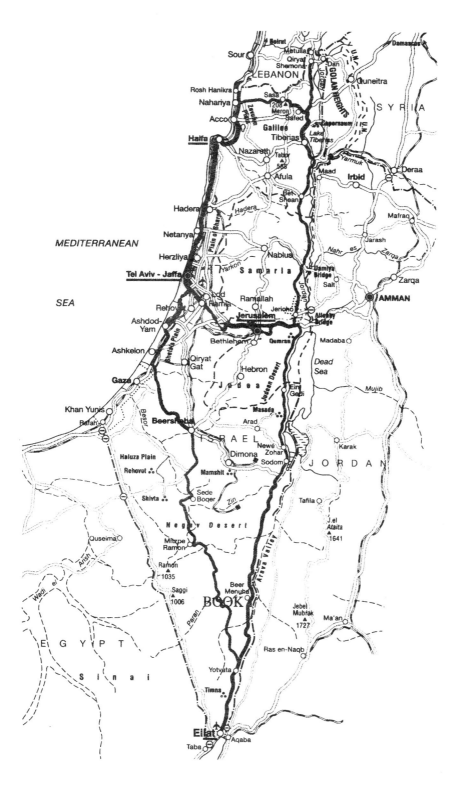